DO CLAIM THE TEMPTING ATHLETE

Jewel Family Romance

CAMI CHECKETTS

Birch River
Publishing

COPYRIGHT

Do Claim the Tempting Athlete: Jewel Family Romance

Copyright © 2020 by Cami Checketts

All rights reserved.

No part of this book may be reproduced in any form or by any electronic or mechanical means, including information storage and retrieval systems, without written permission from the author, except for the use of brief quotations in a book review.

FREE BOOK

Sign up for Cami's VIP newsletter and receive a free ebook copy of *The Fearless Groom: Texas Titan Romance* by clicking here.

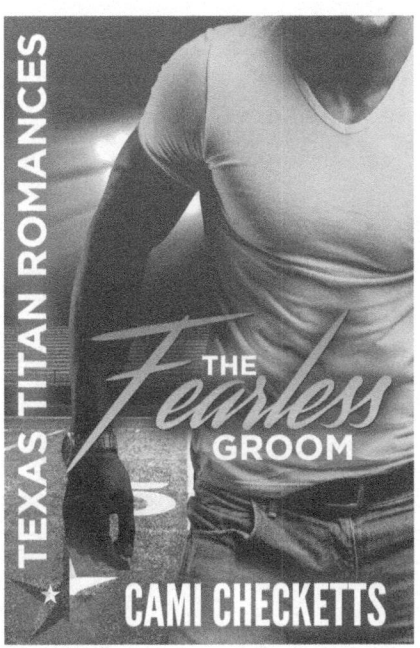

CHAPTER ONE

Eve Jewel bent low and kissed her daughter Paisley. "I'll come get you for lunch in three hours," she promised.

"Okay, Mama. I'll be having the time of my life doing my work." Her blue eyes lit up as she winked with more sass than any four-year-old should possess and sauntered away to join her friends at Eve's gym's play center. Eve always felt a sting of guilt for leaving her daughter while she worked but Paisley loved the gym's daycare and the workers all adored her.

"Don't worry about her," Abbie, her play center manager, said. "She's the happiest little girl and everybody loves her."

"Thanks, Abbie. I just hate missing out on any time with her."

Abbie nodded with understanding. Her own daughter was now at the daycare with her, but she used to work as a receptionist at a local dental office and had to leave Shay every day. Her husband had MS and worked from home. Eve knew they were struggling financially and her husband wasn't healthy enough to help much with their little girl. Eve paid her as generously as she could.

"I know how that goes," Abbie said.

Eve raised a hand, watching Paisley organize a game in the play kitchen with several other children.

She backed out of the play center's door, having a hard time taking her gaze off of her darling girl. Though Eve still dealt with disappointment with herself and resentment against Mark for charming her into thinking she was in love at eighteen, whisking her away to Vegas, and immediately getting her pregnant, all the while planning on stealing the inheritance she wouldn't receive until twenty-five—she'd never regret having Paisley. Her little girl was the best part of her life.

She ran into someone as she backed out of the door. Whirling, she found herself face to chest with a well-built man. "Oh, excuse me." She glanced up and the oxygen sucked from her lungs as she stared into perfection. The man had blue eyes that could rival the Jewel family's eyes in brightness and clarity, as well as a well-trimmed beard that complimented the strong planes of his face. He was smiling at her and the deep dimples in his cheeks, visible even through the facial hair, softened what would have been a face far too much like she'd always imagined Apollo would look like.

"Sorry I didn't see you," he said, holding his phone up. "Texting and walking."

"Should be illegal."

He slipped his phone into the pocket of his shorts and leaned even closer to her. "Eyes as pretty as yours should be illegal."

Eve's stomach hopped happily at the compliment but she forced herself to not fall into the trap of *his* beautiful eyes. "Empty compliments will get you nowhere." She surprised herself by saying the line much too flirtatiously with a welcoming smile that clearly told him she wanted more empty compliments. Her sister, Rachel, and her sassy sisters-in-law would be proud. They always gave her a hard time about never giving any handsome man a chance to flirt.

"It wasn't empty," he insisted. His gaze seemed sincere, but what did she know? After her one failed attempt at a relationship, she'd focused on getting through college in under three years while also being pregnant and having an infant and then toddler underfoot.

When she graduated, she searched the country for the perfect spot to raise her little girl, then secured a loan from her dad to buy this gym in Golden, Colorado. She'd almost paid that loan off in the past two years. She loved her gym and her work as a personal trainer.

She lifted her eyebrows in an obvious challenge, compliments like that were always empty and were usually the prelude to an even more empty and meaningless dating fling. A single mom didn't have the time or energy for that kind of relationship.

She backed away then spun on her heel and headed toward the weight room. The main floor of her gym housed a two-story massive weight and cardio room, the state of the art locker rooms, the daycare center, racquetball courts, basketball courts, and indoor pools. Upstairs, the areas that weren't open to below housed separate rooms for aerobics, spin, and Pilates/yoga, as well as personal training rooms, offices, and a juice bar and deli.

She heard him walking behind her but chose not to stop. She had a personal training appointment that she was already pushing being late to. There were always plenty of fit and handsome men in her gym—she knew how to stay strong. Raising Paisley was her priority. Sure, she got lonely, but she had a great family to support her and interact with when she needed adult communication.

She'd almost made it to the weight room when he touched her arm. Spinning, she folded her arms across her chest. "Can I help you?" She said it pleasantly. Eve rarely got snippety with anyone, but she didn't have time to flirt.

He nodded. She would've thought he was a very serious guy if his blue eyes hadn't been twinkling. With his tall, muscular frame, maybe six-four or five to her five-eight, and that mischievous glint in his eyes, he reminded her of her brother Caleb, about ready to play a prank or "sturdy trick" on someone.

"Yes, ma'am. I'm new to the gym and wondered if you could show me around?" He glanced down at the fitted t-shirt she had all of her employees wear. The Fitness Spot emblazoned on her chest.

"Oh, shoot! I'd be honored to, but I have a personal training appointment at nine. I'll find someone else to give you the tour." He should've already received an in-depth tour when he signed up for the gym unless her employees weren't doing their jobs. But she was certain her employees were doing their jobs. It hit her—he was trying to get more time with her. She shouldn't have been so irrationally happy that he was being obvious about it.

"Don't do that. I'll lift some weights while I wait for you."

"I have an appointment at ten also."

"Popular trainer."

Eve lifted her hands and shrugged. What was she supposed to say? She tried to turn as many clients over to the other trainers as possible but many people insisted on her and then they told their friends about her. She got results and didn't waste time and many people appreciated that.

"I'll lift until ten-forty-five, shower, and meet you right here a few minutes after eleven."

"Do you always get what you want?" she asked, partially annoyed he wouldn't take no for an answer and partially impressed at his tenacity.

"If it's something I really want." he shrugged. Even though she was surrounded by muscular bodies every day she was impressed with the strength and definition in his shoulders.

"And a tour of the gym with me is what you really want?" she challenged.

"Yes, ma'am." His voice came out deeper and made her heart race faster.

Eve smiled at him and shook her head. "Fine. I'll see you right here a few minutes after eleven."

"Right here?" He pointed at his feet, his dimples growing deeper as he grinned at her.

"Not an inch to the left or the right," she shot back.

He chuckled, tilted his chin to her, and sauntered past her to the free weights. Eve kept her mouth closed but she let herself watch him walk away. He looked good, really good. Was he an athlete of some sort? He was like a walking billboard for fitness. She was glad he'd chosen her gym.

Suddenly, she felt someone standing next to her. Eve turned to find her client. "Trudy," Eve greeted her warmly. "Ready to work?"

Trudy was staring after the man. It was then that Eve realized she hadn't even asked his name. She needed to shift into trainer and owner mode when she gave him the tour. It was time to stop flirting and start being friendly but professional.

Trudy's mouth was slightly open as she watched him pick up sixty-five-pound dumbbells and start with lateral raises.

"Trudy?" Eve questioned, passing a hand in front of her face.

Trudy blinked but didn't stop staring. "Do you *realize* who that is?"

Eve shook her head. She let herself look and fully appreciate the striations in his arms as he lifted. She liked that he wore a comfortable t-shirt and not a ripped-up tank like some guys did, trying to show off. It was still more than apparent how muscular he was. "Tough guy with a nice face?"

Trudy rolled her eyes. "Nice? You call that manly beauty and absolute perfection, *nice*?"

Eve laughed. "Maybe it's more than nice. Let's get you warmed up." She directed her to an open area with mirrors and mats and started her on inchworms.

Trudy glared up at her as she performed the exercise. "Only you would insist on inchworms when I could be staring at Beckett Tanner. What is that beautiful man doing in Golden?"

Eve glanced over at the object of Trudy's drool. Beckett Tanner. It fit him. She liked it. She was dying to beg Trudy for info. Who was he? Why was it surprising he was in Golden? Golden was a cool town,—only twenty miles west of Denver, nestled against the mountains, a beautiful spot with a trendy downtown, and with a river running through it. She loved this town. Even more so now that Caleb and Luke each lived less than thirty minutes away with their wives.

"Plank," Eve instructed Trudy.

"For the love of men, let me at least do something standing up so I can gawk at him."

Eve laughed and shook her head. "Okay, squats."

"Thank you," Trudy breathed. Trudy had never thanked her for any exercise before. She was a matter-of-fact thirty-year-old who worked hard but didn't gush about much of anything. She squatted deep with perfect form but her gaze was focused on Beckett, who was now doing an overhead press. Eve glanced around and it seemed like half of the late-morning crowd was goggling at Beckett as well. She rolled her eyes and focused on her client, pushing her through an intense workout. The entire time, though, her gaze strayed to Beckett almost as often as Trudy's did.

Several times she caught him looking at her. He'd give her a dimple-revealing grin before returning to his exercise. He was definitely appealing, tough, handsome, and he'd been fun to tease but she prided herself on the fact that she wasn't begging Trudy for information about him—no matter how badly she wanted to.

Trudy finished twenty burpees and dropped onto the mat, sweaty and obviously exhausted. "Let me catch a breath," she begged.

"Sure. Then twenty pushups," Eve said.

Trudy groaned. She rolled over and stared up at Eve. "You seriously don't know who Beckett Tanner is and you aren't even going to grill me with questions?"

Eve's eyebrows lifted and she shouldn't have but she glanced over to where Beckett was currently using the cable machine for a triceps pulldown. Whew! Those triceps were nicely formed, popping beautifully for her to gawk at.

"I've noticed him checking you out," Trudy said before she rolled over and started into pushups. Eve felt her face flush. Trudy had noticed too? She put a hand to her cheek and forced herself not to look at him again.

Trudy finished her pushups and Eve couldn't think what she was supposed to do next. Trudy glanced up at her. "Eve?"

"Um ..." Her mind raced but all it could see was Beckett, smiling at her with those blue eyes and those dimples that showed even through his short facial hair. Why did he try to cover up dimples that beautiful? Who was he that had Trudy so interested? Well, Trudy was probably interested because he was so good-looking but he must be famous too. She should be thinking about how great this was for her gym, but all she could think about was how great it was for her personally.

"How about we do some rows on the cable machine?" Trudy grinned up at her.

Eve gave a very uncharacteristic giggle.

Trudy jumped to her feet. "Let's go." She raced across the weight room, fluffing her short, dark locks with her fingers as she went.

Eve followed her client. What choice did she have? There were two cable machines placed side by side. One was empty. The other was occupied by Beckett.

Trudy reached the machine and moved the pin to ninety pounds. Eve lowered the handle and traded out the bar for the rope, hyper-aware that Beckett was close by. Was he staring at her? Was he thinking it was her idea to race over here? Not that had she minded, but she didn't want to look like she was chasing him.

She straightened and Trudy grasped the rope just as Beckett finished his own set of rows, released the rope, and glanced over at them. When he caught Eve's eye, his polite smile turned into a full grin. "Hey," he said in a deep, throaty voice that made her warm all over.

"Hey," she managed, lifting a hand.

Trudy released the cables and put one hand on her slim hip. "Beckett Turner, as I live and breathe. Hello." She stuck out her hand.

Beckett extended his hand and shook hers. "Nice to meet you, Ms. ..."

"Trudy Gunnell." Trudy grinned and licked her lips. "Very nice to meet you. What brings you to Golden?"

"I have a home here," he said evasively. He glanced past her to Eve and also extended his hand. "Nice to meet you, Ms...."

Eve figured she couldn't be rude to a client of her own gym. She put her hand in his and felt a strength and peace radiate through her. This was a man who would be there for her. This man would never ditch her when he found out she hadn't received an inheritance from her father. She startled and would've pulled her hand back to stop her crazy thoughts but he held on to her hand and stared at her, waiting, waiting for what?

"Your name," Trudy hissed, making her feel like a complete idiot.

"Oh ..." Eve blushed furiously. "Eve Jewel. Nice to meet you."

Beckett held onto her hand. "Beckett Turner, but you can call me Beck."

Trudy sighed beside her.

Eve pulled her hand back and focused on Trudy. "Rows," she said.

Her client rolled her eyes but grabbed the rope.

Beck smiled and nodded to them both. "Bye, Trudy," he said.

"Bye," Trudy said breathlessly.

"See you at eleven," he said to Eve, focusing his blue gaze on her and making her knees feel wobbly.

"See you," she said just as breathlessly as Trudy.

He strode away to the free weights area and neither woman moved as they stared after him.

"That is a perfect specimen," Trudy murmured.

Eve shook herself from the Beck-staring trance and adjusted the weight on the cable machine. "I think you can take a little more weight on the row but take it nice and slow."

"You don't agree that he's a stud?" Trudy asked, turning back and taking the rope from Eve to start executing the row.

Eve shrugged. "I'd prefer not to objectify him."

Trudy chuckled. "Stay on your high horse and I'll drool and objectify." Her mouth twisted in a frown. "If only he'd look at me like he does at you."

"What do you mean?"

"Please tell me you're not that closed off to the male species. I've heard how men ask you out and you claim you can't date clients. But come on ... Beckett Tanner was checking you out hardcore. Oh, wait ...

he asked *you* to call him Beck." She winked. "Give that handsome man a chance, for me if not for yourself."

Eve couldn't resist darting a glance at Beck. He looked in the mirror and caught her gaze, giving her a grin that she felt was meant only for her.

She bit at her lip and turned away as Trudy muttered, "Point proven."

CHAPTER TWO

Beckett Tanner tried to focus on his workout but it was near impossible with the gorgeous trainer in the same weight room. He'd stared at her as he lifted and occasionally was rewarded with her meeting his gaze and gifting him with her incredible smile before she glanced away. The other woman with her had no such innocence, staring brazenly at him. Beck was used to that, being a well-known NHL player, the only heir to his eccentric grandpa's fortune, driving a two-million-dollar, one-of-a-kind car, and being featured on far too many magazines claiming he was "the most eligible bachelor", and other such bunk. All of this complied together had brought him more attention than he wanted from women of all ages. Just yesterday a fifteen-year-old had hit on him at a sandwich shop. He'd kindly told her he couldn't go out with her because he was old enough to be her father. Not quite true, but the encounter had still made his stomach turn.

He focused on a lateral raise as Eve said goodbye to her nine o'clock client and started into a warmup with her ten o'clock training appointment. This client was a man, close to Eve's age. A well-built guy who was probably attractive, if Beck were to classify another man as such. His eyes narrowed as the guy said something and she smiled sweetly, revealing slight dimples in those smooth cheeks.

Beck felt a possessiveness flair in him that was both unfamiliar and undesirable. He didn't want to feel jealous when he hardly knew Eve, and the interaction between her and her client was most likely innocent. The guy brushed against her and Beck straightened, ready to throw gloves. Instead, he dropped to the mat and pumped out twenty pushups. It was better if he couldn't see them but a light, tinkling laughter floated to him anyway, causing him to feel weak and hot all over. Eve's laughter. He knew it as well as he knew his own hockey stick. Her laugh was as sweet and appealing as the rest of her.

He glanced up at the clock. Ten-forty. He wouldn't mind lifting longer but he'd told Eve he'd be showered and ready to meet her for his tour at eleven. It would probably be better for him not to shoot daggers at the man Eve was training anyway. It wasn't as if he had any right to be by her side.

Checking her position one last time, disappointment surged through him. She was so focused on her client, touching his back while he executed deadlifts, that she didn't even glance Beck's way. He knew trainers often touched their clients to remind them to keep proper form but he still didn't like seeing Eve touch another man. He headed for the locker room, responding to some female greetings as he went, wishing Eve was simpering over him as so many other women did.

Looking around he was impressed with the clean, spacious locker room. There were various hot tubs, a steam room, and heated tile beds in the relaxation area. He headed for the showers, enjoying the private spacious shower with a therapy head. His shower at home was nicer but this wasn't anything to complain about. Maybe he'd lift from nine to eleven-thirty every day until the regular season practices started in August. He could shower here and see if he could talk the beautiful Eve Jewel into lunch each day. It was early June so he'd have two and a half months to try to get her to fall for him before he had to be at practice and team workouts in Denver, not hanging out at the hometown gym.

He left the shower, got dressed, and looked at himself in the mirror. He was being a little obsessive about this woman that he didn't even know—worrying about her laughing with another man, thinking how he'd talk her into dating him, planning his day around spending more time with her.

He straightened his shoulders and studied himself. His mom had taught him to be humble and not get too high on himself. She always used to say: "You're blessed to be talented, smart, handsome, charming, and wealthy. And by darn you'd better be a humble hard worker too, or I will *break* you." He smiled to himself, thinking of her shaking her slim finger at him as she said it then laughing and hugging him, dissolving any concern of her claiming she'd "break him".

He brushed his hair and his teeth and then stowed his stuff back in his locker, dropping his cell phone and wallet in his pants pocket.

He was Beckett Tanner. It was time he listen to his mom's voice, stand up tall, and show this lady exactly who he was.

Striding confidently from the locker room, he spotted Eve standing alone across the open foyer of the gym, next to the stairs. She turned his way and her gorgeous smile lit up her blue eyes. He felt like he'd been slammed into the wall and somebody was jabbing their stick into his solar plexus. Beck was immediately humbled, ready to grovel for any attention she'd toss his way, and uncertain that any man on earth was worthy of such a woman. It wasn't just her external beauty, she radiated a sort of calm and peaceful feeling that seemed to speak to his soul.

He stumbled across the foyer as if it were his first time on skates, but he was on solid ground. Reaching her, he smiled like a besotted sixteen-year-old. "Hey."

"How was your workout?" she asked.

Completely pushing his luck, he rested his hand against the stair railing and leaned in closer to her. She looked up at him so sweet, so radiant, so incredible, he knew he had to get to know her. What good was being a successful hockey star and an heir to billions if he couldn't date the woman of his dreams? He hadn't even known she was the woman of his dreams until he saw her two hours ago.

"I struggled," he admitted.

She leaned back against the stairs and stared up at him. Those blue eyes sparkled like sapphires. Did he know any poetry about blue eyes looking like precious stones? Maybe he could make something up about her being a jewel like her name. Would she laugh at him if he started spouting poetry? What was happening to him? His teammates would be laughing themselves silly if they knew his crazy thoughts.

"Why's that?" she asked.

He wanted to touch her so badly, brush her long ponytail over her shoulder or touch the smooth skin of her cheek, but he knew he had to slow down. Simply because he thought she was incredible didn't mean she felt the same. "There was this exquisitely beautiful personal trainer with the most intriguing blue eyes," his voice was low and husky and she hardly blinked as she stared up at him. "She stole all of my attention and made it difficult for me to focus on my workout."

Beck held his breath, hoping he had some favors left with his favorite guardian angels— his parents and grandmother. Hopefully they'd send some good vibes down from heaven and nudge Eve toward him.

Eve blinked up at him and then snapped her fingers. "Ah, Melissa is a doll." She inclined her head toward the weight room. "Would you like me to introduce you?"

Beck leaned closer, inhaling her clean, sweet scent. "I am *not* talking about Melissa," he murmured. Didn't she realize he couldn't even see another woman with her filling up his every thought?

Her eyes traveled over his face and his hopes rose, but then she slid away from him and the staircase and walked toward the weight machines. "We'll start our tour with the weight room. You seem to know your way around the equipment."

Beck groaned but followed her. The tour was much quicker than he would've liked and Eve didn't rise to any of the flirtatious bait he tossed out there. She was friendly but professional. They finished their tour back in the foyer near the staircase where it had started.

"Well, that's it," Eve said, spreading her hands. "Any questions?"

"Would you please to go to lunch with me?" he asked before he could stop himself.

Her eyes softened and warmed but just as quickly a shutter seemed to cover them. "I'm sorry," she said. "I have a standing lunch date."

His stomach dropped. "I can't compete with this 'standing lunch date'?" he asked bravely.

She gave him an almost flirtatious smile. "You're cute, but nowhere near as cute as my lunch date."

With that she headed for the stairs, tossing her hair back over her shoulder. "Thank you for choosing to join the Fitness Spot. We're thrilled you chose to work out here and hope you'll love our gym."

Beck watched her go, feeling confused and frustrated. This probably wasn't the time to admit it to himself but he couldn't think of a woman who'd ever turned him down, ever. He also wasn't trying to be big-headed but other gyms he'd worked out at had been ecstatic to have the walking billboard of a professional athlete choosing their gym. They had often gushed over him almost to the point of embarrassment. Eve had acted very... unimpressed. It was possible she had no clue who he was, which was fine. But... he wanted to impress her and to win her away from whoever her standing lunch date was. He was nowhere near as cute? Ouch.

He went to retrieve his bag from his locker and slowly walked out into a beautiful June morning. The trees were all green and full. Clear Creek was choked with late spring runoff. He walked the block down to the river and sat down on a bench to think, staring at the roaring water.

A standing lunch date? Cuter than him? She didn't think he was as attractive as her date. That stunk. Who did she go to lunch with every day? A friend, a boyfriend, a ... husband? Horror rushed through him. She was married. She hadn't been wearing a ring but women often didn't at the gym. It was the only thing that made sense. And he was cuter than Beck... much cuter.

He pushed a hand through his hair, sick to his stomach. She was married. Reaching down, he picked up a rock and hurled it at the rushing water. Of course she was married. There were enough smart men in Colorado to assure that a woman as perfect, sweet, and intriguing as Eve Jewel wouldn't just be sitting around single, waiting for Beck to show up and convince her to date him.

There was one way to find out. Ripping out his phone, he Googled Eve Jewel. Some pictures of her came up and he withheld a sigh of longing. What was happening to him? Sadly there wasn't much information, almost as if she worked to stay out of the spotlight. There were a lot of pictures, social media posts, and articles about her siblings. Caleb Jewel played lacrosse for the Denver Outlaws and had been framed for murder a year and a half ago. Joshua and Luke Jewel were both wealthy and in the spotlight a lot. Two of the female Jewel in-laws owned *Cosette*, a successful perfume company. Seth Jewel was an X-games star on dirt bikes and snowmobiles. Eve's sister Rachel had been burned in an explosion and received a lot of attention about a year ago.

The only real information he could find on Eve was a few pictures of her with her siblings, a video of her telling off the media after Rachel had been injured, and a little clip from the local paper, the Golden Transcript, about her buying the Fitness Spot. So she owned the gym? Interesting. And very impressive. She seemed young to own a gym, which made it even more impressive. There was nothing about a husband and Jewel looked to be her maiden name. She and her siblings all shared the same brilliantly blue eyes. He started relaxing a little bit, at least he hadn't gotten crazily invested in a married woman. Yet she could be engaged or dating someone seriously. What was a "standing lunch date" anyway?

His phone rang, distracting him from stewing over Eve. He stood and started to walk the mostly-shaded river trail, sliding his phone on. "Papa," he greeted his grandfather.

"Beckett. My boy," Papa's voice boomed back. "Are you well?"

"Always, sir. And you?"

"I'm old, cranky, I hurt all over, and my doctors are ticking me off." He grunted with disgust.

Beck held back a laugh, barely. Always the same with his grandpa. He was always real. Beck loved it. "Sorry to hear it, sir."

"Don't get old," Papa warned.

"I'll do my best, sir." Beck chuckled.

"Don't make fun of me," Papa warned even more sternly. "Now I don't have time to waste, so listen up."

Beck always smiled when he said that. You'd think at eighty-eight Beck's Papa would slow down, but he was still heavily involved in his various mortgage brokerages and he also liked to be well-informed on politicians so he could decide in his mind who was honest and doing their best for the people and then he'd throw insane amounts of money at them.

"You turn twenty-seven in August."

"Yes, sir."

"I want you settled down and married before your birthday."

"Married?" Beck yelped and stopped walking, facing the river. "Excuse me, sir?" His grandfather had been opinionated through the years about Beck's education and upbringing. He insisted on Beck not being spoiled, "growing up to be a Tanner", and being a hard worker, but he'd never indicated that he wanted him married. His dad was an only child and so was Beck so there were a lot of expectations placed upon him, but not like this.

"You heard me, don't act all shocked."

"Well, sir, I wouldn't mind getting married someday." Eve's face flashed through his mind. He'd been yanked in by her calm confidence. The peace that radiated from her really spoke to him, an anchor he could appreciate and was drawn to since losing his parents. "But why don't we set a reasonable time frame? Thirty sounds like a good round number." Didn't all those silly movies about a man having to get married set thirty as the deadline? Maybe in three years and a couple of months, the right woman would stride across his path. Maybe Eve Jewel was that woman, but he wouldn't know that in two and a half months. Marriage was a serious, huge commitment.

"No!" his grandfather shot back. "I've been praying hard to Grace and your parents and I feel all inspired. My angels have spoken. I'll be dead soon and I want you settled and happy before I join your dad and mom and my Grace. Twenty-seven's a good number, you've got over two months and some pretty determined angels on your side, do your part and get to work."

Beck was shaking his head. He often felt his parents and grandmother's spirits close by as well, but none of them would support Papa in this kind of craziness. Trying to force him to get married before his next birthday? Papa had never shown signs of dementia but apparently it was manifesting itself. "No, sir. I love you, Papa, but I'm not rushing into marriage to appease you."

"If you don't, I'll give each of my companies to their respective CEOs."

"Good, they probably deserve them anyway."

"And," Papa continued as if he hadn't spoken. "I'll donate all my individual properties, including the family homes, the jets, and *all* of my investments and savings to ..."

Beck waited for Papa to say which cause those billions of dollars and assets would go to. Had Papa already researched a worthy cause? When he didn't speak up, Beck felt a rush of hope. He wouldn't receive the money for his own foundation, and it would stink to lose his family homes and all those memories, but he could still help many children.

"Papa," he said earnestly. "I've done a lot of research on the best children's charities that give close to a hundred percent to the children. Would you like me to send you the lists I've compiled?"

"No," Papa's voice was stern and unyielding. "I have a charity I'm going to give it to if you don't get married. Save the Hyenas."

"Save the Hyenas?" Beck asked incredulously. His dreams of helping dashed again. "Is that really a cause?"

"I saw it on Facebook," Papa declared. "Just looked it up again when you decided to be an ungrateful whelp and not get excited about getting married like I know you should. Save the Hyenas is legit."

Beck returned to his walk along the river trail but it was more of a storm. "Whatever," he said angrily. "Do whatever you want with your money, you earned it." Beck didn't need the money. He earned a great salary with the Colorado Avalanche and he'd been investing in stocks and mutual funds since he'd started cleaning his dad and granddad's offices back in elementary school. He had millions of dollars in various investments and a great home of his own.

The only problem was he had spent a lot of time researching and he'd known exactly what he was going to do when he received all his family money, billions of dollars in assets, property, and liquid cash. He had it all mapped out to donate everything but the family homes and the jet to his favorite children's charities, saving only enough to start a foundation of his own. Every year from the time he was ten-years-old until her death three years ago, his mom had taken him on a church humanitarian mission and they'd always chosen to work in orphanages or be with children. His foundation would focus on trips like that, working with churches to find worthy volunteers who had the desire but not the means to help. His foundation would provide everything they could for the workers and the children in need.

It had hurt too much to go without his mom these past few years so he'd focused on helping children locally. But he'd dreamt of using all that money to further his mom's dream and help the little children he'd fallen in love with on those trips. They were innocent, happy, and loving, even if they had so little food their bellies hurt, slept in the dirt, or didn't have a family to love them. He wanted to bring needed love, attention, and relief to those kids.

It wrenched something deep inside him to take away the dream of helping so many children, almost like having his mom ripped from him again. It would also sting to say farewell to the homes in Newport Beach, California; Tuscany, Italy; Victoria, Minnesota; and Kauai that he'd grown up in. He had so many great memories with his parents in each of those places.

The least important thing was the jet, but if he was honest with himself, he'd still miss having a private jet at his disposal. The Boeing 747-8 was one of the most luxurious jets in the world and Beck loved it. But at the end of the day it was his granddad's money and the man could do what he wanted with it. Papa always did exactly what he wanted anyway, Beck didn't know why he'd gotten his hopes up. *Please say he's joking about the hyenas*, he prayed.

"Beckett! Don't you say 'whatever'. Don't you dare take that tone with me," Papa demanded.

"You're the one telling me I have to get married in two months. That's insane."

"Well, you do. I feel it deeply, and don't you tell me it's insane. You've had enough of this playing around, dating for fun, being the hockey superstar, driving around in your Bugatti like you're the king of the world. It's time for you to settle down with a beautiful angel, like my Grace, and have a passel of kiddos. Don't be stupid and only have one like your daddy and I did. That one might disappoint you."

Beck rolled his eyes. He and his father had both worked hard to surpass Papa's expectations, but he loved to throw out barbs like that if Beck wasn't doing exactly what Papa thought he should. As he stormed up the asphalt trail, he missed the beauty of the trees and Clear Creek, which was more of a river than a creek in his opinion. He tried to smile at the children on bikes and scooters as he passed and not just plow right past them.

"I'm serious about this, Beckett."

"I don't doubt you are, sir, but I don't believe you'll give your fortune to Save the Hyenas. Who even likes hyenas? They're the villains in Lion King." He tried to keep his tone light, but he was peeved. His grandpa could and would give his fortune to the hyenas, or almost as bad, to politicians who told him what he wanted to hear. It was still Papa's money and his choice, but Beck also had a choice. The old man had no right to tell him to settle down. Papa had gotten married at thirty-nine after seeing the world, and securing his fortune. Grandma had been thirty-eight, a retired actress. Their age was the real reason they'd only had one child. He wasn't sure what his parents' excuse was. His mom used to say when you'd created the perfect child, who wanted to tempt fate again?

His mom. She would side with him on this one, maybe. She'd actually told him once she wanted him to not wait too long to get married. She'd told him to find the right one and have lots of babies for her to spoil. Too bad she and dad had been killed three years ago in the small propeller plane Dad loved to fly.

"It's the hyenas, or you married and happy. I promise you I'll make those hyena lovers happy if you're not going to be."

"I believe you, sir." His grandpa was both determined and full of integrity. He didn't make empty threats. Though he believed in tough love, he usually didn't throw around too many threats. Beck truly did love the guy and would miss his last family member when he passed. He was just supremely annoyed with him right now.

"I know you're a bleeding heart, Beckett. All those trips with your mom to orphanages and the videos she sent to me showed how you lit up around the kids, how happy helping them made you. Nowadays you're always participating in some charity event to help the children, bringing a kid out on the ice to make their day, and other junk like that. It's admirable. I love it about you, son, that tenderness for little ones. And now I'm going to use it against you. Would you truly rather the hyenas get *your* money instead of all those children you could help?"

Beck gripped the phone tightly. The hyenas. His stomach tightened in anger. His grandfather would do it too. If Papa wouldn't use all that money to help children couldn't he at the very least choose dogs or penguins or an animal that people *liked?* Hyenas. Sheesh, he was getting more and more eccentric every day.

"Sir, I can't get married in two months. I'm not even dating anyone." Again Eve's beautiful smile and incredible blue eyes appeared in his mind but she hadn't even seemed interested in him and for all he knew she was already married or engaged.

"You can and you will. I'm getting the will changed. Don't push me on this."

Beck had no response. Papa had made up his mind. Beck would honestly try to find someone. It wasn't that he was opposed to marriage. He'd been dating since he was fourteen when he realized he liked girls, a lot. He just hadn't found that certain someone he wanted to spend the rest of all eternity with over the last twelve years of dating. How was magic going to happen in the next two months, no matter what Papa insisted that his angels had told him? Insanity. His grandfather had officially lost his mind. It was horrible, but Beck wondered if he could challenge the will. The children in need definitely deserved all that money over the stupid hyenas.

He reached the point where the trail split, going over a bridge or arching up the other direction toward the small college. He took the bridge option and then headed back down on the opposite side of the river, past the city's water supply.

"Beckett?" Papa sounded tired. "I wouldn't do this if it wasn't for your own good."

"Papa ..." Beck tried to reason with him. "Rushing into marriage is not smart. You've always taught me that it's a forever commitment. I need time to find the right person, to date long enough to make sure she doesn't have any issues."

"That's the problem, right there. You young men wanting to find some perfect model. *Everybody* has issues, everybody has junk hiding in their closet, but if you love the Lord, love each other, and have the guts to commit to something besides hockey, you'll be just as happy as Grace and I were, as your mom and dad were."

"My mom and dad dated for years before they married."

"That's cause your dad was stupid and slow and had commitment issues. I could go on, but don't make me badmouth my own blood about how he was a wimp about marriage. Grace and I dated three weeks and knew it was right. Married a month later and happier than anybody had a right to be."

Beck was passing the RV park now. He'd love to stay here with his own wife and family, right on the river with a park nearby, and head up into the mountains every day for hikes, but he had to find that wife first. Everybody had issues? Well, that was probably true, but he wanted the right woman for him with issues that Beck could handle.

"Papa, it's not like I don't want to be married."

"Not sure I believe that one. I've seen the pictures of you with empty-headed, big-chested, hair-color from a bottle, redheads."

"Papa! You can't judge women like that."

"Who's gonna stop me? Two months and ten days to find your woman Beck, or the hyena supporters are going to be howling like hyenas." He laughed like a hyena at his lame joke and hung up.

Beck slid his phone into his pocket as he stormed down the trail toward the lower bridge, back into town and to his car. Married in two months or the hyenas got the inheritance he'd hoped to use to help millions of children.

If only Eve Jewel was available and interested in him. He shook his head and pounded across the bridge. For the first time since his sixteenth birthday—when the old man had told him he had a big present for him and walked him slowly through his glistening shop full of dozens of beautiful Bugattis, Lamborghinis, and Maseratis then cackled as he handed him the keys to a twenty-year-old, rusted-out Civic—he really hated his grandfather.

CHAPTER THREE

Eve saw lots of glimpses of Beck Tanner over the next week at her gym. He caught her eye and gave her inviting glances often as she was training a client, but she'd been booked back to back throughout each morning and hadn't had a minute to approach him before he disappeared about eleven-thirty each day and she always went to lunch with Paisley at noon.

She woke at four-thirty a.m. every day, did her own weight or cardio workout in her small home gym, which was ironic as she owned the best gym this side of Denver, but she didn't want to be away from Paisley any more than she had to. Then she'd shower and work on responding to emails, marketing, or bookkeeping for the gym until Paisley woke up. They'd have breakfast together and head to The Fitness Spot.

Usually after lunch, she might have one or two more personal training appointments but she'd focus her time in her office upstairs of the gym on employee issues or training and whatever else she needed to wrap up for the day. By three or four she and Paisley would head out to spend the rest of the day together.

She'd Googled Beck that first night she met him after Paisley had fallen asleep. Even the pictures of him online took her breath away. When she realized he was a star defenseman for the Colorado Avalanche, an heir to billions, and looked like a superstar popping out of his beautiful car in pictures, it made more sense why Trudy, and it seemed every other woman in the gym, couldn't keep their eyes off of him. That wasn't completely fair though. Beck would've probably received all of those longing glances simply because of how attractive and fit he was. Plus he really appeared to be a nice guy, not a cocky gym rat. She'd noticed him helping people with equipment, joking with young men who looked at him with idol worship, and even helping one of the older ladies to the pool area for her therapy workout. It was an honor to have a professional athlete and weight-lifting advertisement like him at her gym. She wanted to gush about him and to him, but that wasn't her personality, at all.

Eve found herself becoming obsessed with the man, watching for him at his usual workout times between nine and eleven-thirty, Googling him after she put Paisley to bed and watching videos of him playing hockey—he was singularly impressive on the ice—and unfortunately seeing numerous pictures of him with a lot of different women, often helping them into that gorgeous navy blue and silver car of his. He seemed to prefer redheads with generous bosoms. Dang. Her dark hair did have natural copper highlights but she was sadly lacking in large chest measurements, too thin and muscular her mom would say.

A week after she'd first met him, she was walking backward out of the daycare after dropping off Paisley when she ran into someone solid. Whipping around, she felt her stomach give a happy lurch when she realized it was Beck.

A warm smile lit up his handsome face. "Hey," he said.

"Hey yourself." She felt her own smile growing.

"You've been busy," he said. "First time I've seen you alone in days."

"You've been waiting to catch me alone?" She arched an eyebrow, her stomach hopping happily.

He nodded.

Eve wanted to question him about why he'd want her alone but she wasn't very proficient at flirting. She was trying to remember the last time before she met him that she had even cared to flirt. "Here for your daily abuse?" she asked.

He nodded. "Gotta stay in shape for hockey season."

"Oh... you play hockey?" She tried to play it cool and not reveal she'd Googled him far too often since he'd appeared at her gym.

"I've been known to skate a time or two." He smiled as if he knew exactly how obsessed she was becoming with him.

"That's... nice." She was an idiot. Nice? He was spectacular, intriguing, impressive, mind-consuming. Nice?

She turned and started walking toward the main area and the weight room. She was training Trudy at nine o'clock. Beck fell into step beside her. She glanced up at him. She loved that he was as tall and built as her brothers. It made her feel like he could protect her from the bad things in the world—mostly Mark showing up again. During her pregnancy, she pushed through as much schooling as she could before her daughter was born. At times she'd fought loneliness and even longed for Mark to reappear. Now she hated him completely and dreaded the thought of him coming around and possibly seeing Paisley. She'd worked hard to stay off of social media and away from any paparazzi that tracked her family, to protect Paisley from her weasel of a father.

"Do the team trainers orchestrate your workouts?" she asked.

"They send suggested workouts in the offseason but they don't own us until we go back to practice the end of August."

They entered the open gym foyer with the skylights above the two stories and the focal point of the staircase. Trudy was walking in the front doors.

Beck put a hand on her arm and Eve stopped walking and stared up at him. He leaned slightly closer and lowered his voice, "Are you married?"

Eve's eyes widened. Why would he ask that? Was this the time to tell him she had been married? For one long, horrific week. "No."

"Engaged?" His blue eyes were intent and she felt like she was being interrogated. She wished she knew his motive.

"No."

"Dating someone seriously?"

"Hey you two," Trudy trilled out. Eve hadn't even heard her approach, so focused on Beck and his questions. She stared into his beautiful blue eyes and wondered: Did he want to date her? That would make sense why he'd be asking these questions. Her heart threatened to beat out of her chest and she couldn't hide a happy smile.

Did Beck know she had a daughter? Would he be interested in her if he did? She'd been asked out a lot since Paisley had been born, and even more often people tried to set her up with their neighbor, cousin, brother, etc., but she was focused on her daughter and hadn't been tempted to date. She was tempted now. What would dating look like with a rambunctious almost five-year-old in tow? She was getting way ahead of herself. Just because Beck was asking her personal questions and looking at her so intently didn't mean he'd want to date her.

Trudy cleared her throat and Eve finally tore her gaze from Beck. "Hey... sorry."

"Hi," Beck said, raising a hand.

Trudy looked back and forth between the two. "No worries." She gave them a knowing smirk. "I can warm up by myself. Give you two a minute to finish..." She swirled her finger between the two of them, "whatever this is." She winked and walked away.

Eve blew out a breath and glanced back at Beck. "I need to go."

He nodded. "I understand but... can you answer my question first, please?" His voice lowered. "I've been dying to know for a long, lonely week."

Eve smiled, though if the online pictures were accurate at all, this man was rarely lonely. "I'm not dating anyone."

He let out what sounded like a breath of relief. "I forced myself not to be the stalker-type and made myself leave every day at eleven-thirty when I wanted to wait around and see who you went to lunch with. If you're not dating anyone, who do you have a 'standing lunch date' with?"

Eve bit at her cheek. He was interested in her. It was thrilling but terrifying. What should she do about it? "Do you want to know?"

He smiled and nodded. "I do. I really do."

Eve was nervous but she wanted to be brave. She tried to be as brave as her amazing older sister Rachel who conquered her fears of showing her scarred face to the world for the man she loved. Eve took a deep breath and said, "Why don't you meet me right here at noon and I'll introduce you?" This was big. A man she was intrigued by was going to meet her daughter. This hadn't happened in... wait, this had never happened.

Beck nodded quickly. "I'd love to meet... your lunch date... I think."

"I think you'll like her."

His smile burst through. "It's a her? Oh, man." He chuckled. "I've been tormenting myself over the past few days and thinking I should stay away but not wanting to and..." He pushed a hand through his hair. "A her is nice."

Eve was getting an adrenaline rush better than jumping off a cliff at Lake Powell from simply talking to him, knowing he was interested in her and had been "tormenting himself". "She is a nice girl, but also... sassy."

"I can handle sassy."

"We'll see." She smiled and tilted her head toward where Trudy had gone to warm up. "I'd better go."

"I'll be waiting right here at noon."

"Not an inch to the right or the left," she teased.

He chuckled. "I'm memorizing this spot."

She grinned, lifted a hand, and hurried to Trudy.

"Whoo-ee, girl, you are the luckiest woman this side of the Mississippi."

Eve pushed at her ponytail. "It's just lunch." And with her four-year-old, hilarious but also unpredictable daughter. How would Beck react to her having a daughter? If he wasn't great about it, she'd simply walk away with Paisley. She glanced at him and realized walking away would already hurt.

"Well make sure you make it more than 'just lunch', Trudy advised.

"I'll try my best." Yet Eve not only wasn't an expert in flirting she wasn't sure she should be meeting Beck for lunch. Life was good for her and Paisley: simple, fun, safe from Mark and the media— there were no complications. A man like Beck Tanner would definitely complicate life.

She looked up and he was squatting with a barbell loaded with forty-five-pound plates. It seemed like their eyes were drawn to each other as he straightened out of the squat and stared right at her. Her stomach hopped and her cheeks got hot. He met her gaze with the most appealing smile. Complicated? Definitely. Worth it? She didn't know yet.

Beck waited by the staircase, exactly in the spot he'd been earlier this morning, just as Eve had instructed. He smiled greetings to other gym-goers passing by. It was almost noon and he was going to lunch with *the* Eve Jewel. He was as nervous, excited, and happy as a rookie playing for the Stanley Cup.

He'd gone the rounds with himself the past week—wanting to wait for her after her training appointments, wanting to stalk her and see who her lunch date was with, wanting to pull a favor from the realtor who'd just helped him find his house in Golden and find out where she lived and then stake out her house. He'd forced himself to calm down and give it some time. He was still peeved at his grandpa and he didn't want to pull Eve into that situation, which he realized was a little messed up. He should be begging her to date him, seeing if she could possibly be the right one and moving on quickly to date someone else if she wasn't. A little over two months and the hyenas got the fortune instead of needy children. Beck refused to get married if it wasn't right, no matter where the money was wasted. His grandpa was such a...

dipwad sometimes. Dipwad wasn't strong enough but he was trying to quit swearing, at least in the offseason.

He didn't want to mess up what could be something beautiful with an incredible woman like Eve by worrying about his approaching birthday and the guillotine hovering over his neck.

Forcing those troubles away he thought about beautiful, sweet, intriguing, irresistible Eve. He could hardly wait to spend time with her. It was only lunch, and someone else would be with her, a close friend he'd assume. He was definitely, definitely taking advantage of this opportunity to spend time with her. Hopefully he could win the friend over and she'd help him in his pursuit of Eve.

It made him shake his head at himself that he'd been torturing himself the past week about her "standing lunch date" and it was with another woman. A sassy girl. Beck smiled again. Despite the angst over the situation with his grandpa, he felt lighter and happier than he had since hockey season ended, no, since before he lost his parents. The anticipation of being with Eve was like waiting for Christmas morning. He'd have to focus on the friend as well, include her in the conversation, make her feel important so she liked him and encouraged Eve to date him. There was a fine balance though, under no circumstances did he want Eve to think he was interested in her friend. For some reason, every other woman had fallen to the wayside and it was all Eve for him. Had Papa planted these seeds with his angels directing him to force Beck into marriage, or were his parents watching out for him above and had set Eve in his path right when his Papa made his insane marriage demands?

He sensed movement behind him and spun to stare through the open staircase toward the back hallway. Eve walked toward him, smiling shyly, and carrying a little girl, maybe four or five. The child was a beautiful, miniature Eve. Eve was a mother. It hit him hard yet also took a second for the truth to sink in. Eve was a mother. This darling child was her standing lunch date. No wonder she'd said her date was much cuter than Beck.

A myriad of questions followed the reality of the situation settling in. How old was Eve? Where was the father? Hours ago she'd told him no husband, no fiancé, no boyfriend, right? Did she have support from her semi-famous family, friends, a church group, her ex, or was she raising her daughter all alone? Would she let Beck help her? Okay, he needed to slow down and not scare Eve off but this was just about perfect in his mind.

Eve's gaze was apprehensive as if she were worried if he'd accept her daughter. She shouldn't worry about that. His grandpa had been accurate about how much Beck loved children. He cared so much for children he'd most likely end up married in the next two months, simply so he could help millions of hungry and neglected children with all of that money. Children energized him, made him laugh, could make him happy even when he was desperately missing his parents or dwelling on the fact that he was all alone in this world besides his teammates and his grandfather, and that cranky old grandfather wasn't going to be around for much longer. Beck would rather spend time with children than anybody in the world, well with the exception of Eve.

She walked up to him and Beck grinned at the little girl and extended his hand. "I'm Beck Tanner. It's a pleasure to meet you."

The dark-haired, blue-eyed child grinned impishly, revealing soft dimples. "You have dimples in your cheeks. That's funny!"

"So do you," Beck said, gently poking one.

She giggled louder then reached out her hand. "Paisley Jewel. It's a pleasure to meet you."

Beck laughed and shook her soft little hand. "Is she four or fourteen?" he asked Eve.

"I'm almost five, thank you very much." Paisley pushed out her lower lip.

"Apologies, Princess Paisley. Of course, you're almost five."

"Princess Paisley." Paisley lifted her thin shoulders and grinned. "Yes!"

Eve smiled at him and hefted Paisley higher on her hip. "You've started something now."

"I hope so." He opened his arms. "Can I carry you, Princess Paisley? You're almost as big as your mom."

Paisley wrinkled her nose, looked him over, and flung herself at him. Beck caught her easily, holding her in the crook of one elbow. She was much lighter than he thought she'd be. "Which restaurant are we going to for lunch, your highness?"

Eve let out a soft groan next to him but when he looked at her she was smiling softly at the interaction.

Paisley's eyes widened and she looked from Beck to her mom. "We get to go to a *restaurant* for lunch?"

Eve started walking toward the front door and Beck glanced around, noticing some patrons and employees watching them. Eve must not be wanting everyone to gawk at their interaction, or maybe she didn't want anyone to know she was dating him. Dating was stretching it but that's where he hoped this was heading. He'd been nothing but impressed by Eve and now to find out she had an adorable, sassy daughter?

"Yes," Eve answered her daughter as they reached the front door and Beck hurried to push it open and hold it with his free hand so Eve could walk through first. "We'll walk to a restaurant close to the gym."

Walking was good, for some reason he wasn't ready to reveal his two-million-dollar Bugatti to Eve. He liked how unassuming she was and didn't want to scare her away by his very attention-grabbing car.

Paisley clapped her hands together happily. "Can I have grilled cheese?"

"Sure, love."

Paisley grinned up at Beck. "I love me some grilled cheese, all gooey and delectable. Scrummy."

Beck burst out with laughter. What four-year-old said delectable and scrummy? Wasn't that British slang?

"Delectable? Scrummy?"

"I told you." Eve shook her head. "Sassy."

"That's me," Paisley chirped.

"Where did you learn 'scrummy'?"

"My Uncle Luke and Aunt Mar took me and Mama to Park City to snow ski. We got to meet Heath and Hazel Strong. Do you know them?"

He shook his head, no.

"Well they're the bestestest and Hazel is an English lady, and she says scrummy so I say it." She shrugged her thin shoulders.

They walked along the sidewalk as Paisley chattered like she was a teenager. Beck assumed it was hanging out with adults all the time that made her so mature.

The sun was high and bright but it wasn't too hot, maybe seventy. With Eve by his side and Paisley cradled in one arm, her skinny arms wrapped around his neck as if he were her father, Beck felt more like a champion than he had when his team won the Stanley Cup. His thoughts were racing out of control, wanting to know about Paisley's real father, but instead of grilling the obviously-private Eve with questions he asked, "Where to?"

"We like Café 13. They have a light lunch and delicious salads."

"Perfect." Light lunch? He could order a couple of meals or eat again later if he needed to. No reason to explain he didn't do any "light" meals. "What do you normally eat for lunch, Princess?" he asked as they walked down Main Street.

"Peanut butter and jelly on high-protein bread with lots of veggies on the side," she said. "I like it, but grilled cheese on bad-for-me white bread is better."

"For sure." Beck snuck a glance at Eve. She seemed comfortable being by his side and with him holding Paisley.

Paisley talked about the benefits of grilled cheese versus peanut butter and jelly as they entered the light-filled café, ordered, and Eve headed for a booth in the corner, glancing around quickly as if to make sure no one was watching them. Beck found that interesting, but he didn't mind being alone with her. Eve didn't say much but Paisley made up for any shyness on her mother's part. Was Eve shy or simply reserved or horrifically not interested in Beck? He tried not to think about it too much and focused on the little girl telling him all about her famous Uncle Caleb who played lacrosse for the Denver Outlaws.

"I love lacrosse," Beck told the little girl. "I think it's a tough, fun sport to watch but I've never been to an MLL game or played it myself. Can I go to a game with you sometime?"

Paisley's eyes lit up but Eve looked a little... concerned. Beck was going to have to take this slow. Sadly he didn't have the luxury of slow. Not if he had any hope of meeting his grandpa's demands. What if his grandpa truly had an inspired premonition he'd meet someone like Eve? Maybe being married in two months wasn't insanity. He pushed that drama out of his mind and focused on the two beautiful ladies with him.

"For sure!" Paisley cheered. "Then you could meet Aunt Emily and Krew. They're the bestestest."

Beck grinned, wondering if everybody was the bestestest. He wanted to meet Eve's family. All of them. Large families had always fascinated him but it was more than that with the Jewel family. He wanted to know more about Eve through her family.

Eve's Thai chicken salad, Paisley's grilled cheese and fruit, and Beck's chicken street tacos and Reuben sandwich arrived quicker than he wanted them to. He wanted to extend his time with these two. He remembered his manners but ate and chewed quickly so he could talk with Eve more. Paisley was fully focused on her food and giving these cute little moans with each bite. Maybe Beck needed to try grilled cheese out again. He couldn't remember the last time he'd eaten one.

He leaned closer to Eve. "How's the salad?"

"Delicious. Would you like a bite?"

"Sure." It was beautifully intimate as she took his fork from him, stabbed some chicken, lettuce, green onion, peanuts and dressing on the fork and actually fed it to him. He liked the Thai flavor and the chicken was really good but he preferred his Reuben sandwich to the salad or his tacos.

"It is delicious." His eyes lingered on her mouth as he said it. "Would you like a bite of either of my meals?"

She smiled and shook her head. "No, this is much more than I would normally eat for lunch."

"What would you normally eat for lunch? Peanut butter and jelly?"

She smiled and looked at Paisley who'd set her sandwich down and was stacking her fruit like a pyramid. "No. I have a cheese stick, almonds, and 'lots of veggies on the side'." She smiled fondly at her daughter.

"Every day?" Beck asked.

"Except for Sundays."

"How do you not starve to death?"

She shook her head with a smile. "I have a lot less mass to maintain than you."

"That's for sure."

They each took a bite and then he got brave and asked, "What would it take for me to get a blanket invite to your 'standing lunch date'?" He paused and she didn't respond right away. "We don't have to go to a restaurant every day if you prefer a cheese stick and 'lots of veggies on the side'." He winked. "I could bring a picnic, get you your cheese stick, and Paisley her peanut butter and jelly. Whatever you want." He realized he was sounding a little desperate so he stopped, and waited, and waited.

She took a drink of her water and met his gaze. "You're okay with me... having a child?"

Beck nodded, surprised that she would even question if he was okay with Paisley. The little girl was hilarious and sassy and cute. "I think she's great."

Eve's gaze slid to Paisley who had shoved a large bite of watermelon in and was chewing happily, liquid dribbling down her chin. Eve dabbed her daughter's chin with her napkin and then ate another bite of her salad. Beck was about going insane waiting for her decision. As she quietly ate her salad, he forced himself to resume eating but for the first time since the weeks following his parents' tragic death, he'd lost his appetite. What if she didn't answer him? What if she wasn't interested in him or she was so protective of her daughter that she wouldn't bring an unknown man into her life?

They finished eating, cleaned up, left a tip, and were walking back to the gym before he dared ask again. Paisley was skipping slightly ahead of them. Beck put his hand on Eve's lower back. She sucked in a breath and her eyes darted to his. She looked apprehensive but also affected by his touch. He felt strong and brave like he'd just scored a hat trick, simply being close to her and touching her warm, firm back.

"About that standing lunch date..." He let it linger, hoping he wasn't pushing his luck. Maybe he needed to give it a few days, keep giving her flirtatious glances at the gym, and hopefully finding time to talk with her to get her more comfortable with him. It had to be a large act of trust to allow an unknown man to be around her daughter, especially with how private he sensed she was.

Eve seemed to lean a little closer to him. "I think it would be okay if you were included."

Beck punched his free fist in the air. "Yes!"

Eve laughed softly. "I take it that makes you happy?"

"Very."

"Why do you want to be with us so badly?"

"Have you looked in the mirror lately?"

Eve drew a little bit away from him and Beck knew his answer hadn't been the right one. There were many reasons he wanted to be around this pair. "But it's not just about how beautiful you are," he rushed to say. "You have a very calming, intriguing personality and Paisley is adorable and fun."

"Sassy," Eve said.

"That too. I've only recently moved to Golden and most of my friends are in Denver and most of my teammates are traveling during the off-season and my parents died three years ago so..." He cleared his throat, knowing he'd gone too far. He wished he hadn't admitted that to her. He wanted Eve to want to be with him because he appealed to her, not because she felt sorry for him.

"You're lonely," she said quietly, compassion making her blue eyes even deeper.

He hadn't realized he was lonely, that his dates lacked meaning and he was searching for the connection to family, the connection he'd lost when his parents died... until he met her. "Yes," he admitted. "But it's more than that. I'm drawn to you and I think Paisley is great. I'd love to spend more time with both of you."

She tilted her head. "It's surprising to me that you'd be lonely with all the pictures I saw of you with redheads and all the attention you get from women everywhere you go. Why choose a single mom who doesn't care to date or flirt?"

He kind of liked that she had Googled him, but it was the first glimpse of jealousy and lack of confidence he'd seen in Eve. She was obviously reserved but she had this innate self-assurance that seemed to shine from her. It may have been from her impressive family, her faith in a higher being, or simply being beautiful and successful her entire life. Whatever it was, he wanted to restore it and quick.

"I'd choose you every time," he said sincerely and earnestly. "Because you're the most intriguing, smart, beautiful, and at peace woman I've ever met. Please let me spend more time with you and Paisley." *I don't want to go another day of my life without seeing you, hearing you laugh, fighting for the chance of securing a touch, or in my happiest dreams a kiss.* Whew, he was in deep and quick. Was this his angels in heaven pushing or simply how incredible Eve appeared to be?

Eve pursed her lips, not seeming impressed with or swayed by his compliments. Paisley ran back with a dandelion. "I picked you a pretty, Mama."

"Thank you, love." Eve took the flower and bent to give her daughter a kiss on the cheek. A surge of desire rushed through him. Not simply physical desire, though that was part of it. With Eve it was only part of the picture though. He desired her spiritually, emotionally, mentally, and physically. From the little he'd seen, she was the entire package to him. He wanted to be near her and Paisley, wanted to see if he could be part of their lives. He said a quick prayer to the good Lord and his parents and grandmother. *Please let her give me a chance.*

They all walked to the gym doors and Beck still didn't have an answer. No woman had made him work like this, especially not for a simple lunch date. He was about ready to ask again, make a complete simpering fool of himself, when Eve turned to him and said, "Standard lunch date. We each take a turn paying and choosing the place, or bringing a picnic. I'll bring a picnic tomorrow."

Beck was thrilled with her declaration but wanted to argue about the administration of it. His family may have been old fashioned but his parents had taught him to be a gentleman and he wanted to woo her with how chivalric he could be. He might need his impressive car and maybe some videos of him playing hockey to sway her to him.

He sensed now was not the time to argue so he simply nodded. "I can't wait for my cheese stick and peanut butter and jelly."

She actually laughed. It was light and happy and as beautiful as the rest of her. Paisley laughed as well, though she obviously didn't know why they were laughing. "I'm glad you're a simple man," Eve said.

"For you, I could be just about anything," he said in what he thought was his charming tone.

That wiped the smile from her face. "Lunch date," she reminded him. "No empty flirtations, no one-night stands."

Beck's eyes widened, he wasn't interested in a one-night stand, but he only said, "It wasn't empty."

She stared at him. "We'll see." Then she took Paisley's hand and hurried toward the gym. "Thank you for lunch."

"Thank you," Paisley chirped.

"Of course, my princess," Beck said to Paisley.

She giggled. Eve gave him one more serious, almost concerned glance and then they disappeared inside the gym. Beck was smitten. Too bad Eve didn't seem to feel much of anything toward him. Winning her heart would take a lot of work. He walked slowly to his Bugatti, wondering if he was willing to work so hard because Eve and Paisley were so incredible, because Eve was a challenge unlike other women who rushed to be in his arms, or because his grandfather's ultimatum was hanging over his head. He definitely didn't want to marry an empty-headed woman like his grandfather had claimed he always dated. His grandfather and Eve had referenced him always dating redheads. He was drawn to them, but Eve's dark hair glowed with copper highlights and he'd never been so invested in any woman. He suspected he'd already fallen head over heels for Eve. Sadly he doubted in two months that she would return the favor.

CHAPTER FOUR

Eve couldn't say that Beck scared her. The fact was he downright terrified her. And not simply because he was famous and might bring the media down on her, exposing Paisley to online pictures, and possibly leading to Mark finding them. It also wasn't that she feared Beck would hurt her or Paisley physically, but he could destroy them both emotionally. She couldn't shake the feeling that she was just a challenge to the impressive, playboy hockey star and as soon as he won her heart he'd move on. Paisley was young enough she'd probably heal okay and someday forget how fabulous Beck was. Eve didn't know that she ever would.

Eve sometimes wondered if she could claim she was healed from her ex. No matter how pathetic that made her, as Mark was not worth any of the pain he'd caused her. Was she insane to let another man into her heart? Maybe. Was she completely lame to be thinking so seriously about Beck when all they'd had was one lunch date? Probably.

Paisley talked of little else that night or the next morning but her new friend, Beck. To hear Paisley tell it Beck was as strong as Uncle Isaac, as funny as Uncle Caleb, as smart as Uncle Josh, as brave as Uncle Seth, as "hot" as her newest Uncle Abe, and he smelled as good as Uncle Luke. Luke smelled incredible because his wife Mar and Isaac's wife Cosette owned their own perfume company. All the other descriptors fit too. Oh my, Eve and Paisley were both in trouble.

Eve couldn't help but think it was adorable how smitten Paisley was with the tough, impressive, confident, handsome, and obviously successful Beckett Tanner. Yet what would happen to both of them when he found another large chested redhead to date? Eve felt instant guilt for being jealous of every well-endowed redhead.

She packed a huge lunch for Beck, using high-protein bread, lean turkey, cheese, avocado, and lots of fresh veggies on the sandwiches as well as nuts, cheeses, and veggies for side dishes while Paisley ate her breakfast and prattled on about Beck. It was hard to not get completely enamored herself, simply from the way he looked at her with those incredible blue eyes. Paisley falling for him so quickly made it even more difficult.

It bugged Eve that she was suddenly lacking confidence and thinking she couldn't possibly be the woman a man like Beck Tanner would pursue. Men stared at her, flirted with her, and asked her out all the time. It wasn't as if she didn't know she was attractive or desirable. Sadly, Mark's desertion always reared its ugly head and made her doubt her value as a wife to anyone, as well as doubting the sincerity of every man besides her brothers and dad.

She pushed it all away as she loaded Paisley and the lunch into her Cherokee and drove the short distance to her gym. She loved her beautiful neighborhood on the west side of Golden—she'd always felt safe and welcome there. Her house was a gorgeous two-story colonial. It felt good to have bought her own house, to have almost paid off her gym, to be successful without her five million dollar inheritance that would come in eighteen more months. Mark had married her for that five million dollars, then dropped her like a hot rock when he found out she wouldn't get it for seven more years. Served them both right. She'd been stupid and naïve, not listening to the Holy Spirit's gentle caution or even giving her family a chance to warn her away as none of them had ever met Mark. Mark was a selfish jerk and the signs had been there but she rushed in thinking she was in love. But she had got Paisley out of it and that was all that mattered.

She walked hand in hand with her daughter into the gym, kissed her goodbye, and hurried to meet her first appointment. Beck came in a few minutes later than usual. He caught her gaze and gave her an irresistible grin. She couldn't believe how much she loved dimples on a man. They had the effect of softening his otherwise completely manly, tough, handsome, incredible face.

"Eve?" Her client, John, was staring at her, and then he easily followed her gaze to Beck.

"Oh, sorry." Her face and neck heated up as she realized he'd completed an exercise and she'd been distracted by ogling Beck. "Lateral raises. Forty-fives, please."

He obediently grabbed the weights and slowly lifted but his dark eyes seemed troubled. He was a nice guy, an accountant in Denver about her age. He'd asked her out and she'd explained that she didn't date clients. That one always came in handy.

"You do realize he's dated every redhead this side of Kansas?" John gritted out as he strained to lift the weight.

Redheads. There they went tormenting her again.

"I'm not that into social media," Eve said. Usually, she wasn't into social media. She'd looked at it plenty since she'd met Beck. "Shelve the weights and twenty burpees please."

He arched his eyebrows but obeyed.

Eve let her gaze wander to Beck again. He was using the cable machine for upright rows but her stomach dropped as she saw a gorgeous redhead in tight, ultra-short shorts flirting with him. Eve looked away quickly. Redheads. She'd never felt much jealousy in her life. In high school, she'd had plenty of boys after her then she'd fallen hard and fast for Mark on her senior trip and married far too young and quick. After that, she'd cut herself off from dating completely and focused on Paisley. She didn't like feeling all jealous and grumpy and wanting to sneak into redheads houses at night and dye their hair black. Oh, my.

She concentrated on her client and somehow got through until noon. She hurried to pick up Paisley from the kids' care. Rounding the corner to the back hallway she sucked in a quick breath as she saw Beck waiting for her, leaning casually against the wall. He looked simply... incredible. His golden-brown hair was brushed away from his handsome face. His dimples were on fine display. His blue eyes twinkled happily as if he could hardly wait to spend time with her. Eve's stomach did a little flip. Was this really happening? Was she ready? Could she trust him? She knew most men were great guys, unlike Mark, but her ex had done a number on her.

"Hey." He pushed away from the wall and strode quickly to her. Reaching her, he tenderly swept her long ponytail off her shoulder. "I've been waiting for this lunch like a four-year-old waiting for his first hockey stick."

She smiled. "Because that is every child's desperate wish."

He shrugged. "The smart kids."

She laughed and Beck's face lit up. "I love your laugh," he said, his voice deep and sexy.

He leaned closer and Eve's eyes widened. What was he doing? The more important question as she found herself arching up while he leaned down: What was she doing?

Beck's gaze traveled over her face as tender as any caress and then his large palms cupped her cheeks. Eve shivered with anticipation and delight at his warm, tantalizing touch and the smoldering look in his blue eyes. He could look at her all day and she wouldn't complain. As he lowered his head and their lips were moments from connecting she decided he could look at her all day, after he kissed her good and long.

"Mama! My Beck!" Paisley's happy voice rang out from behind them.

Beck whirled around and away from her, and Eve hurried to take Paisley from Abbie's arms.

"Sorry," Abbie whispered, her face flaring red. "Paisley said she saw you and you always come at noon and so I walked her out..." Her voice trailed off as she stared at Beck. "Wow. You really are Beckett Tanner."

Beck smiled and extended a hand. "I really am. Nice to meet you..."

Paisley launched herself at Beck. He easily caught her, giving her a huge grin and a hug before transferring her to his left arm and shaking Abbie's hand.

"Abbie Lower. My husband's a huge fan. So huge. I took him to a game for his birthday present last year and they treated us so nice, probably because of the wheelchair and..." Her voice trailed off and her face turned red again. Abbie did not like to draw attention to her difficulties.

Beck's face filled with compassion but he kept his big smile as he said, "I'm so glad to hear that. Is he a fan of anyone particular on the team?"

"Mostly you."

"Ah, I love it." Beck nodded. "I'll get you a jersey and some tickets for next season if you'd like." He seemed to sense how embarrassed she was.

"Oh, you don't have to." Abbie tugged at her shirt. "But he'd love it."

"I'll bring them tomorrow. It was great to meet you."

"You too." She waved to Eve and Paisley. "See you in an hour, pretty girl." Abbie disappeared back into the daycare.

Beck looked down at Paisley, pulling a funny face. "Doesn't she know you're Princess Paisley?"

Paisley giggled. "It's okay. I can be pretty and a Princess."

"Ah, that is true. You're definitely both." He winked at Eve. "Both of you are."

Eve felt heat rush through her. Since Mark she hadn't allowed herself to be swayed by honeyed tongues or empty compliments, but Beck had told her twice his compliments weren't empty. The scary thing was, she believed him.

Beck rested his hand on Eve's lower back and escorted them out through the gym. Eve tried to ignore the interested looks they got. Sometimes she worried that his popularity would bring social media attention to her and Paisley. Luckily it was the off-season and Golden was a laidback town, no paparazzi hiding to expose the handsome hockey player and his latest date. Was that all she was? His latest date.

She pushed those worries away and focused on the heat his hand created on her back. She couldn't remember a man's touch feeling this incredible, but maybe she'd just been out of the dating game too long.

"Thank you," she said to Beck as he swung open the gym door and they walked out into the sunshine. "That means a lot to Abbie."

He nodded. "Is her husband paralyzed?"

"MS."

He pulled in a quick breath. "She's so young."

"So is he. Their little girl, Hannah, is adorable, only two."

"Wow, that's rough. I'll bring season tickets, a jersey, and a bunch of other junk."

"Thanks." She led him to her car, popped the back, and pulled out the small cooler and another sack of non-perishable food.

Beck tugged the cooler from her hand. Paisley prattled on about what games she'd been organizing and playing this morning with her friends as they walked across the river to nearby Lions Park.

Eve laid out the food on a vacant picnic table in the shade. It was perfect as it was out of the way, the playground blocking someone seeing them from the road or parking lot. They wouldn't attract attention, but they could easily watch Paisley on the playground. Paisley quickly devoured her peanut butter and jelly sandwich and went to play on the slides and climbing equipment nearby. Eve had only picked at her turkey sandwich but Beck had devoured two large sandwiches, all the nuts, a high-protein yogurt smoothie, and a bunch of veggies. He was like her brothers, loved and demolished food.

Paisley was close enough that Eve could hear her girl's cute chatter with the other children, but she also felt almost alone with Beck. She lost all her brave and focused on her lunch and her daughter, basically ignoring him even though they sat side by side at the picnic table. It was June fifteenth tomorrow and the table was only partially shaded. Sweat trickled down her back. She wasn't sure if it was from the heat or the feelings the man sitting next to her stirred in her.

"Eve," he said softly then waited until she looked at him. His blue eyes were warm on her face. "Thanks for letting me be part of your standing lunch date."

"Of course. Sure." She wondered if she was a rotten mom. She always loved time spent with Paisley but the past two lunch dates had been the most exciting lunches she'd ever been part of. Was she simply craving adult interaction? That didn't make her an uninvested parent, right? If only she had somebody to ask. Only Caleb had a child—little Krew who was six when Caleb married Emily a year ago. But Emily and Caleb never seemed to crave a minute away from the adorable Krew. They had taken a two-week honeymoon where the grandparents each spent a week with Krew. She wished she could ask them if they ever felt guilty for wanting time alone together.

"Paisley is a lot of fun," he said, still studying her.

Eve checked Paisley's position, squealing down a slide and then racing up again with her newfound friend. Paisley instinctively trusted everyone and made friends everywhere she went, whereas Eve tended to keep to herself. Did Paisley take after Mark that way? Eve hadn't known her ex-husband well enough to really say. He'd schmoozed her into thinking he loved her, but she wasn't sure if he was naturally friendly like Paisley. She'd hated how he treated some people like waitresses or service workers with contempt as if they were below him. He'd always showered Eve with compliments, which was why Beck's compliments sometimes threw her off.

"You're a lot of fun too." Beck's voice drew her head around again but his words didn't sit right with her.

She gave a derisive snort and was surprised how annoyed she suddenly was with him. Maybe her instincts were off and he was a smooth liar like Mark. "I'm not fun. I'm a too-serious stick in the mud." Those had been part of Mark's ugly, final words to her. She'd also heard plenty of times from Caleb and Seth growing up that she "worried too much" when she'd urged caution as they made homemade bombs and fireworks or did crazy tricks on their dirt bikes, snowmobiles, skis, or wakeboards. All her brothers were very kind and protective of her but she knew it was Rachel who was the fun one.

Beck's blue eyes widened in surprise. "That's not true at all. You do have a calming personality but you're a lot of fun for me to be around. I love how you tease me."

She stared at him, searching for deception. Would he make her fall for him like she'd fallen for Mark and then ditch her when he realized she wasn't a millionaire yet and her dad didn't give handouts? Beck didn't appear to need money but she hadn't suspected Mark did either.

"Thank you," she finally murmured. She liked the way she could tease with him also so maybe that line from him was genuine.

"Why don't you believe me?" he asked in a low voice.

Eve could hear Paisley's sweet voice but she still checked on her before turning back to Beck who was, unfortunately, waiting patiently for her answer. She laced her fingers together and leaned forward, focusing on Paisley not him. "I married young and it didn't go so well. I have a hard time believing any man could be genuine with me."

It was out. She'd said it. If Beck knew the level of trust she'd just put in him by admitting that much he'd be stunned. Eve took shallow breaths and squeezed her hands more tightly together.

"I'm so sorry your ex hurt you," Beck said simply. She looked at him and his gaze was slowly traveling over her. "He was an idiot to walk away from you."

"Because I'm beautiful?" She shouldn't have been so snide about it but she didn't want to just be another pretty face. Mark had only wanted her for her beauty and family money. She didn't want that with Beck, not that Beck seemed to need money but you never knew. His fancy car was probably worth more than most people's annual salary. Maybe he loved fancy toys, was in debt up to his ears, and wanted an easy way out. She pushed those thoughts away, hating that she'd even had them.

Beck was more serious than she'd seen him. "Your physical beauty is only a bonus to the picture that makes up Eve Jewel. You exude a strength, confidence, and peace that I've never seen before. You're intelligent, kind, well-spoken, and even though you don't believe me, you're very fun for me to flirt with." He finally smiled.

Eve looked down at the table, her face flushing with pleasure. "Thank you."

He put one of his hands over both of her joined ones. The joy of him touching her lit her up all the way through. "Thank you for allowing me to be around you. You're an incredible lady, Eve Jewel."

Eve should've and could've returned all the compliments and then some but as it was she could hardly find her tongue. She simply sat there and savored his hand on hers and his closeness until it was time to head back to work. Beck Tanner. She'd never met a man like him. He was almost as impressive as her brothers, and that was saying something.

CHAPTER FIVE

Several perfect weeks passed, perfect in Beck's mind at least. July came and Beck should've been more worried about the approaching August sixteenth deadline, when his family fortune would go to the hyenas instead of children in need, but all he could think about was Eve.

Beck worked out every morning from nine to eleven-thirty, showered at the gym, and then went with his two favorite girls to lunch. A standing lunch date. In the afternoon he'd practice at an indoor skating rink and catch up on emails from fans, sponsorship deals, and his investments. He was still spending his evenings and nights alone unless a teammate or friend called to have dinner, go to a movie, play basketball or tennis or something. He wanted to be spending more time with Eve and Paisley. He wanted a standard dinner date, a standard movie night, a standard go to the ice skating rink, the zoo, the park, the lake, anywhere, he simply needed to be with the woman and girl who had captured his heart.

Friday they had a picnic lunch at the nearby city park by the river. Paisley made friends and played on the park equipment, only eating when Eve insisted she took a few bites. Beck and Eve had time alone to talk about how she started her gym and how he got into hockey, starting ice skating at two years old on the lakes in central Minnesota. They walked back to the gym after their hour together, Paisley holding both of their hands and them swinging her as if they were a young family. They were almost to the gym when Beck got brave. "Hey, I've been thinking."

"Don't do that, it'll hurt your brain," Paisley chirped, her cheeks dimpling.

Beck laughed, swept her off the ground, and turned her upside down. Her pigtails brushed the sidewalk as she squealed. "How's that feel on your brain?" he asked.

Eve grinned beside him. Beck had to work hard to earn laughter from Eve but she smiled easily. He loved her sweet, innocent yet alluring smile.

"Put me down!" Paisley demanded.

Beck swung her over to the grass and laid her down. "How's that?"

Paisley scrambled and reached her arms up. "Throw me, Beck."

Beck complied, sweeping her into the air and tossing her. She couldn't weigh more than thirty pounds. After throwing her a few times, he held her in one arm and said, "You ready to go back to your job?"

Paisley had made sure to inform him that she was in charge of the play center and it was her job to make sure the "little kids" had fun. He loved being around children and helping children, but as an only child with only a couple of older cousins on his mom's side, he hadn't spent as much time around children as he would've liked. Still, he thought Paisley had to be the most amazing little girl and he was falling hard and fast for her beautiful, intriguing mother. Maybe his grandpa wasn't as crazy as he'd thought and the angels had told Papa that it was Beck's time to settle down. He'd happily settle down with these two, but first, they had to start going on dinner dates and somehow he had to get Eve alone and kiss her. That thought made his mouth go dry.

"Yes, sir." Paisley sighed dramatically. "I mean, the kiddos need me, right?"

"For sure."

He glanced askance at Eve, struck by the beauty of her blue eyes, but wimped out and asked Paisley instead, "Hey Princess, do you like going to lunch with me every day?"

"Of course, kind sir." Paisley giggled.

"What would you think about dinner every night together and maybe doing some other fun stuff together like ice skating, swimming, or boating?"

"Yes!" Paisley cheered. "I've always wanted to ice skate!"

Beck couldn't have loved her answer more. He looked to Eve. She was studying him as if she had to ascertain exactly what his intentions were before she committed. Did she not realize how invested he already was in the two of them? Did she think he was only a temporary addition to their lives? How to convince her of just how serious he was. . . If his grandfather had his way, Beck would be proposing soon. If he told her all, would she run from him? It definitely wasn't the most romantic move: "Hey, I think you're great, and by the way, I need to be married in... about six weeks or the hyenas are going to be not just the ugliest and most creepy, but also the richest scavengers on the savanna." No, that little tidbit was something he should probably keep between him and his grandfather. Maybe at their twenty-year anniversary, he could tell Eve and they'd have a good laugh about it. He'd better slow down right now and talk her into dating him first.

They'd reached the gym and they stopped outside the front doors. Beck looked to Eve. "What do you think?"

Her gaze flickered from him to Paisley and back. "You're okay with..." She lowered her voice. "Both of us?"

"Of course." He loved being around Paisley and wouldn't want to leave her out, though there was a part of him that dreamt of getting Eve alone.

Eve blew out a slow breath but finally said quietly, "Okay."

Beck threw Paisley into the air and caught her as she squealed happily.

"I think she said yes!" And he was thinking about her saying yes to a marriage proposal already. He needed to slow down those thoughts before they ran away with him.

"Yay!" Paisley cheered.

Beck set Paisley on the ground, grabbed Eve around the waist, and lifted her into the air. She cried out in surprise and then laughed, a beautiful, light laugh that had his heart soaring with happiness. Paisley laughed with her and Beck grinned.

Eve rested her hands on his shoulders as he held her aloft by her waist. "You're crazy, you know that right?"

"Crazy for you," he said impulsively.

Eve's smile slipped and her blue eyes grew far too serious. "We'll see," she murmured.

Beck lowered her to the ground, concerned all over again. The guy she'd married must've done a number on Eve to have her be so untrusting. Beck pushed the worries from his mind. They were going on a date tonight. Somehow he'd prove to Eve that he'd never betray her and that she was the one for him. It'd only been a few weeks but he felt the rightness of being with these two clear through to his bones. Paisley reached up to him. He picked her up and she grinned happily. He was pretty sure Paisley was on board. Now how to convince her beautiful mother?

CHAPTER SIX

Eve's fingers trembled as she slid into skinny jeans and a blousy, polka dot shirt. Beck had texted to wear pants and bring socks and sweatshirts. She assumed they were going ice skating. She didn't care what he had planned, she simply wanted more time with him, but still, she was scared. The fear infuriated her. Beck was a good man—a great man. She enjoyed being around him and she was learning to trust him. Still, Mark's handsome face made its unwelcome appearance in her mind and she could never forget his parting words, "I never wanted you, only your money. The only reason any man would claim to love you is your family money and your pretty face because you're the most boring stick in the mud I've ever been around."

She swallowed hard to keep the ugly emotion from choking her. She focused on her face as she put on some simple makeup. Could Mark be right and there were only two reasons a man would want her? Her pretty face and her money? Beck gave her sweet compliments often, but many of them were focused on her calming personality or the fun time they had flirting and simply being together. Did he really think she was fun? He brought out a happy side of her that was different than the happiness she felt with her family and even with

Paisley. She always allowed her siblings and Paisley to be the fun, sometimes almost feeling like a spectator. With Beck, she felt like she was center stage and could soar with the stars. He gave Paisley plenty of attention while still making Eve feel important, valued, and even fun. How did he do that?

The doorbell rang and she heard Paisley yell, "I get it!"

Eve grabbed her phone and rushed through the loft and down the stairs. Paisley was swinging the door wide and screaming, "My Beck!"

Eve reached the landing in time to see Beck lift her daughter into the air, making her giggle. He held her in his arms and Paisley sweetly framed his face and exclaimed, "I'm so excited! This is going to be the best night of my life!"

"I'm excited too." Beck shifted Paisley to his left arm and focused on Eve. "Ah, Eve." He didn't say she was beautiful or anything but she could see it in his gaze.

She smiled. "Hi, Beck. You look great." She meant it too. He filled out a Henley-style shirt and dark wash jeans perfectly.

"Not as great as you."

Eve blushed.

"'My mama's face is like a work of art'," Paisley quoted.

Eve blushed deeper as Beck's eyebrows went up. "That's true, Pais. How does she come up with this stuff?" he asked Eve.

Eve knew exactly where she'd heard it. Some dork coming out of the gym a couple of afternoons ago had been flirting with her and tried to get her to go out with him by saying that line.

"Some yellow-haired guy said it." Paisley shrugged.

Beck's brow furrowed and the look in his blue eyes said he should be the only one giving Eve compliments. She reassured him with her gaze that he was the only one she trusted to compliment her. Beck's face softened and he gave her the most appealing smile. Eve's breath caught. He was proving impossible for her to resist.

"Let's go eat," Paisley demanded.

"Dinner first then?" Beck focused back on Paisley.

"Yes, sir! I'm a starvin' Marvin," Paisley said.

Eve grabbed the backpack with her and Paisley's sweatshirts, socks, gum, snacks, and lip gloss, and walked onto the front porch as Beck held the door. "Nice place," he said.

She nodded. "Thanks. We love it here."

"Do I get the tour later?" Something in his throaty voice brought her head up. Later as in after Paisley was in bed and they could be alone? Surely he wouldn't push her that fast, would he? She hadn't spelled out her trust and commitment issues but this was their first official night date and she was being pretty trusting simply letting him know where she lived. There was no way she'd invite him in and give him the tour. Beck seemed great, but caution with men outside her family circle had become a way with her.

"Maybe in a few weeks," she said.

Beck's eyebrows lifted, but all he said was, "Okay."

Beck easily lifted Paisley's car seat and carried both it and Paisley to his car. He set Paisley down to secure her car seat in the back as Eve gaped at his car. "Are you sure you want to put a car seat in that? I can drive."

He chuckled. "It's just a car."

Eve wanted to argue with him. She'd never seen a vehicle as beautiful as this sleek four-door navy and silver machine. Her brothers would know exactly what kind of car it was. Eve only knew it was pretty, and the man who drove it was irresistible.

They loaded up and drove to Abejas. Beck made sure to get a private table in a back corner, which she really appreciated. Apparently he'd noticed she didn't want the media, or anyone else's, attention. Except for his. She couldn't have imagined a month ago that she would risk media exposure to date anyone, but she couldn't resist more time with Beck.

They ate a delicious meal in the trendy restaurant. Eve had the salmon and it melted on her tongue. She felt a little underdressed, especially when some beautiful women in skintight cocktail dresses rushed to their table and asked for pictures with Beck. He obliged and

Eve kept her smile in place; at least they weren't redheads and at least they weren't interested in pictures of her or Paisley.

Paisley was her adorable self, talking nonstop to Beck, telling the waiter that her grilled cheese was "delectable", and helping Eve relax and enjoy the night. Beck was attentive to both of them and Eve hated how she held back with him. If she couldn't trust a man as kind, open, and impressive as Beck, would she ever be able to trust anyone? It was more than obvious that Beck was invested in the two of them. Why couldn't she let her issues go and trust him?

After dinner Beck took them to an indoor ice skating rink. Paisley was enthralled and so excited as they put on their sweatshirts, socks, and skates. The place was empty besides them and a couple of employees.

"Is it usually this quiet?" Eve asked Beck as they walked awkwardly through the lobby where they'd rented skates for her and Paisley and toward the doors to the rink. Well, she walked awkwardly. Beck was a natural on skates. He looked incredible, so tall and tough and obviously in his element. Even on the squishy lobby floor while carrying Paisley, he didn't so much as wobble. It was just Eve who was waddling like she was pregnant and afraid she'd fall before she even got on the ice.

Beck looked around. "Well... when you rent the place out it's this quiet." He pulled open the door to the arena and cold air stung her cheeks. It wasn't horrifically cold like a Colorado winter but she still shivered.

Eve shuffled through, glancing around at the bleachers and the glass wall surrounding the rink. Beck opened another door and led them onto the ice.

"Do you normally rent the place out?" she asked.

"I've noticed you like things quiet." He shrugged as if it weren't a big deal but it was a big deal, to her.

Her eyebrows lifted but she didn't have time for a follow-up question, or even to thank him, as he escorted her onto the ice and immediately her skates wobbled underneath her. Eve held on to the wall and watched as Beck set Paisley on her skates, bending down and keeping his hands under her arms. "Okay, Princess Paisley. We're going to start skating, but I'll hold onto you."

"Thank you, Sir Beck," Paisley said all sweet and giggly. Eve was glad her daughter was enjoying herself and hoped she could keep a smile on her own face and not end up with bruises all over.

Beck looked over at Eve and his brow squiggled. "Maybe I need to hold on to your mama too."

Eve waved him off, even though she was grateful that he'd noticed and was concerned about her. "I'm fine. It's just been a few years. I'll hold on to the wall and get the hang of it again while you teach Paisley."

Beck looked like he wanted to argue but he simply nodded and skated forward bent over so he could support Paisley. Eve thought it was sweet and Beck was even more appealing to her, sacrificing his back to teach her girl.

She shuffled behind them, slowly remembering how to push off and glide as she kept one hand on the wall in case she fell. She realized some women would've wanted their dates full attention but for her watching Paisley laugh as she skated fully supported by Beck was exactly what she would've requested.

Beck and Paisley glided by several times and Beck would softly encourage Eve while Paisley would remonstrate her. "Go faster, Mama! Let go of the wall, stop being a wimp!"

Eve would simply smile and wave them on. By her second turn around the ice she was gaining confidence and left the wall. Beck and Paisley had stopped flying past and Beck was patiently teaching Paisley how to push off and how to glide. When he seemed to feel she was ready he took her by one hand and as Eve approached them he reached out his other hand to Eve. "I think our Princess has got it. Shall we go together?"

Eve smiled and took his hand. They skated slowly around the rink with Beck as their anchor. They hadn't gone twenty feet when Paisley's feet shot out from under her and she only missed slamming her head into the ice by Beck holding her up with one arm. Beck released Eve, steadied Paisley, and they started out again. Paisley gave a little scream a few seconds later as she must've dug her toe into the ice and she lurched forward. Beck rescued her before she face-planted. Thank heavens for his quick reactions and expertise on the ice.

Paisley ripped her hand free and planted them on her little hips. "I got to do this myself, Beck. You can't be babying me if I'm going to be the Ice Princess."

Beck smiled but his blue eyes were concerned. "Let me hold your hand a few more times around then you can do it yourself."

"No." She stuck out her chin and pushed away from them. Her skates flew backward and she flew forward like Superman.

Eve cried out louder than Paisley did as her daughter sprawled on the ice. Beck got to her quick, lifting her up and checking for injuries.

"I'm okay," Paisley said as Eve hurried as fast as she could on her skates to their sides. Luckily Paisley hadn't scraped anything, though her palms were a little red. "Apparently, I suck at this," the little girl moaned.

Beck laughed, but Eve felt she had to say, "We don't say suck."

"You don't, but sometimes I have to." Paisley stuck her tongue out but Eve didn't reprimand her when she saw the tears in her eyes.

"This was supposed to be the best night of my life. My first date with my Beck and my mama and the whole thing stinks! I'll never be the Ice Princess." She added to the dramatic line by flinging her hand over her eyes.

Eve was trying to think how to encourage her daughter and not make Beck feel badly if Paisley hated ice skating, obviously his passion, when Beck spoke up. "Well, Princess. Sometimes things do suck and sometimes we fall, but what do we do to make it better?"

Paisley stared at him and shrugged. "I don't know. Go get ice cream?"

Eve and Beck both laughed. Beck gave her a happy smile and said, "I love your laugh," before turning back to Paisley. "We will definitely go get ice cream, but first I want you to try a few more times. Learning something new is always hard, but if we keep trying we'll be proud of ourselves for giving our best effort."

"What if I always suck?" Paisley asked.

Beck shrugged. "Then maybe ice skating isn't your thing, but we'll never know if we don't try."

Paisley regarded him as Eve waited. It was a hard balance as a parent, trying to give your child experiences, guide them to be successful, and learn to work hard, without being too demanding or having unrealistic expectations. She liked Beck's approach, try to learn something new, and give it your best effort but there was no shame in it not being "your thing".

Nodding, Paisley said, "Okay, I'm going to keep trying... will you hold my hand?"

"I'd love to." Beck grinned at Eve. "Can I hold your hand too?"

She smiled back and put her hand in his. The warmth and strength of his grip were like an anchor. She realized right then that she not only liked having Beck around, but she was also coming to depend on him, to need him. A dart of fear rushed through her but she ignored it. Beck could be hiding things, he could be lying to her like Mark had, but then again he might be exactly as genuine and wonderful as he seemed to be. She'd never know if she didn't try just like Paisley trying to ice skate. Eve just prayed she wouldn't get slammed metaphorically to the ice and give up completely because it hurt so bad. Her pain would be much worse than a bruised knee or bottom.

The three of them skated slowly around the rink. Paisley had a few more crashes but she kept getting back up and trying again. Eventually, they were skating quicker and more confidently. Eve was proud of Paisley and grateful for Beck and his patience with her girl.

As Beck drove them home, Eve thought about him asking earlier for a tour of her house. She'd said in a few weeks and she thought that might be smart to slow things down between them. Some of her siblings had fallen in love with their spouses quickly but Eve wasn't going to follow that pattern. She needed time and reassurance that Beck was genuine and open with her.

A rebellious part of her hoped Paisley would fall asleep and Beck would have to carry her girl up to her room. Then they'd walk out in the hallway, Beck would lean in, his blue eyes hyper-focused on her and...

"I think she's asleep," Beck whispered as they pulled into Eve's driveway.

Eve's stomach flipped and her heart raced as the fantasies in her mind started to become a reality. She glanced back at her darling little girl, her head lolling to the side in her booster seat. Should she suggest Beck carry her up to bed? Would he kiss Eve after?

Beck put his fancy car into park. Her family had a lot of money, but she didn't think she'd ever been in this nice of a vehicle. He jumped out and hurried around to get Eve's door. Eve slid out and Beck was right there. He was a large man and towered over her, but his size made her feel safe and treasured. She smiled up at him. Maybe he didn't need to carry Paisley to her room for them to have a minute alone.

Beck trailed his fingers through her hair and cupped her shoulder with his hand. His thumb circled along the bare skin above her bicep and delicious shivers filled her.

"Eve," he murmured, leaning closer.

Eve found herself discarding her usually cautious nature as she arched up toward him.

Beck's lips turned up in a slow, appealing grin. He ran his hands down her back, taking his time as if he savored each moment of touching her. When his hands reached her hips, he cupped them and easily pulled her flush against him. Eve let out a soft moan of desire and Beck's eyes deepened to midnight blue. His lips were a breath away and she could almost taste their deliciousness as the scent of mint and his soft cologne wrapped around her as surely as his arms.

"Beck! Mama!" Paisley called from the backseat. "I need to pee!"

Beck and Eve both laughed, though Eve's laughter was definitely unsteady. She'd wanted that kiss, wanted it badly. Beck released her and moved quickly, opening the rear door and getting Paisley out of her car seat. Paisley ran for the front porch. Eve followed her.

"I'll get the car seat," Beck said to their backs.

"Thanks." Eve typed in the code on the front door and Paisley rushed in and for the main floor bath. Eve turned back to Beck as he carried the car seat and her backpack, setting them both next to the front door.

"Thanks for a wonderful night," she said, staring into his bright blue eyes and wanting him to lean down, capture her mouth with his, and push away all her worries about relationships and commitments. Would she know from his kiss if he was fully committed to her?

"Thank you." He rested his hand on the door frame and leaned closer. "Can we make it a standing dinner date?"

She grinned. "If we do I have to pay every other night."

His brow furrowed. "No. I've tried to be forward-thinking and all of that with lunch but dinner is pushing it too far."

She laughed. Beck's gaze deepened and he leaned down so close she could smell his warm cologne. "Thank you for gifting me with your laugh."

Eve swallowed hard. She'd laugh all day long to have him look at her like that.

This was it. It was finally their time. Eve got brave and rested her hand on his chest, savoring the strong muscles underneath his shirt. Beck pulled in a quick breath, gave her an appealing grin, and bent toward her.

Little steps pattered down the hallway then Paisley was pressing against her leg, staring up at them. "Whatcha doing?"

Eve shook her head and stepped back. "I'm thinking it's time for bath, scriptures, and bed."

"With songs," Paisley said.

Eve nodded. "With songs."

"With Beck?"

Eve's breath caught as Beck looked at her so hopefully. She wanted to invite him fully into their lives. She wanted it almost as badly as she wanted his kiss. She simply wasn't ready. More time. That's what she needed. They'd had a great time at lunch the past few weeks, but this was their first real date. She couldn't bring him into her home and have him share in the bedtime routine. A careful mother didn't do that, no matter how amazing the man was.

"Maybe another night," Eve said.

Paisley started to protest but Beck's blue gaze was understanding, even though there was a longing in his eyes as well. "For sure," he said. "I'll see you tomorrow for lunch, Princess Paisley."

Paisley gave a hefty sigh and reached her arms up. Beck bent and gave her a hug then he straightened and surprised Eve by giving her a hug too. He brushed his lips across her cheek and she drew in a quick breath, desire and warmth rushing through her.

Beck smiled as if he knew exactly how he affected her and that she was yearning for more and more of his touches, especially his lips on hers.

"Thanks for tonight," he said. "I'll see you soon."

"Thank you," Eve said.

He backed away and Eve and Paisley watched him go. As he backed out of the driveway in his beautiful car, Paisley sighed, "I love that man."

Eve's eyes widened and she realized how much danger she and Paisley were in. As she got her daughter ready for bed, she prayed in her head, *"Please let Beck be amazing as I think he is"*. The alternative wasn't possible. It would devastate her and her daughter.

CHAPTER SEVEN

Beck, Eve, and Paisley ate lunch and dinner together every day over the next three weeks. Eve insisting on cooking at least half the nights. Beck loved the way she cooked healthy yet substantial, flavorful meals. He complimented her over and over again on any dish she made.

On Sundays, they went to church together and barbecued in his backyard. Saturdays they spent most of the day together at the lake on a boat Beck had rented, in his backyard pool, or at the ice skating rink respectively. Beck loved their time together and prayed he was making Eve feel secure enough to welcome him fully into their lives. Though he'd spent time in her house she still hadn't invited him to share in the bedtime routine, or been alone with him so he could finally kiss those inviting lips.

He had three weeks left until his birthday deadline mid-August. He pushed that from his mind often. As he was getting dressed in Eve's gym locker room on Tuesday mid-morning his phone rang. The screen read Papa Tanner. He smiled but also felt a shot of apprehension. Papa would love Eve and Paisley but he would not understand why Beck hadn't proposed yet. Three weeks to go. The mere thought made him sweat. He hadn't even kissed Eve yet and he wasn't certain he had her complete trust. There was no way he was going to rush their relationship and risk losing the most amazing woman he'd ever met.

"Papa," he greeted him, buttoning his shirt as he rested the phone in the crook of his neck.

"I've been waiting impatiently for a call. Have you found your wife?"

Beck pulled out his hair gel and brush from his locker. "I've met someone, Papa. I think you'll love her."

"I knew it! I've been praying hard to the saints above, mostly your mom and dad, and my sweet Grace. I figured the good Lord was too busy for an ornery, old coot like me but those three had to help out, especially since they inspired the idea in the first place. When's the wedding? I hope before August sixteenth."

Beck pushed out a heavy breath, grateful the locker room was quiet late morning on a weekday. It touched him that his grandpa would pray for him but he didn't think his parents or grandma would want him to rush into marriage, no matter what Papa thought his angels had told him. Even with a woman as amazing as Eve. "About that... I need more time."

"Don't you give me excuses," Papa huffed. "I told you my parameters and I told you I wasn't budging. August sixteenth or you lose the inheritance."

"Papa." Beck set his things on the counter and stared at himself in the mirror. He knew women thought he was handsome and with his success and financial situation he could probably have his pick of women who were only interested in those things. He could probably also look and find dozens of kind-hearted women who would marry him to help the children. He wouldn't do it. He wouldn't settle for anyone but Eve. It wasn't an option. "Eve is amazing but she's got some... trust issues. I can't rush her into marriage. You have to give me more time."

"Time is something neither of us has the luxury of at this point. If she's the right one she'll understand the need to rush."

Beck's temper flared. "I won't do it. I'm not pushing Eve into marriage for your money." And no way did he want Eve to think that was why he was dating her. "Those ugly hyenas can have your billions of dollars."

Beck thought he heard movement from another section of lockers, but he was too focused on his grandfather's stubbornness to pay much attention to anything but the phone call.

"I'm giving it to them then," Papa said.

"Fine. Do it." Beck's gut churned. How could the old man be so stubborn? So many children Beck could've helped. It hurt him deep down, but he wasn't going to marry Eve for money. He hadn't even kissed her. He loved her and he was going to take things slow because that was what she needed. *He loved her*. The thought took him by surprise even though he knew it was true.

Papa pushed out a disgusted sigh. "I'll keep praying you can step up and be a man before August sixteenth. If not, the will is changed."

Beck held on to his self-control, but just barely. "Papa, being a man means doing what's best for those I love, and taking things slow with Eve is what's best for her."

"I've always done what's best for you," Papa contended with him.

"Really? Special ordering me the car of my dreams, but only giving it to me after Mom and Dad were killed? As if the Bugatti could replace them?" Beck sucked in a breath. He'd never even gone there in his mind let alone flung that at Papa.

"You don't know what you're talking about. You think I was trying to replace them? I was just trying to show you how much I love you, not replace them with an inanimate object, no matter how badly I always knew you wanted that exact car. I'd ordered the car a year before they died. It was the only one of its kind and took them almost a year to build it to perfection. I was trying to plan how to give it to you, and then they died. I didn't know how else to show you how much I love you."

Beck heaved out a tired breath. He knew his papa didn't lie or beat around the bush. He appreciated the words but they didn't bring his parents back and they didn't make this marriage push any easier. "Papa. I know you love me."

Silence hung between them for a few seconds and Beck wished he wasn't having this conversation in the locker room of the gym.

"And because I love you I know the time is right," Papa continued. "I feel it. This girl is right. Marry her. Save your fortune from the hyenas. Be happy, my boy."

"Papa, please. She needs more time. You don't understand what she's been through. She needs privacy and to take things slow."

"Time is the one thing you don't have, Beckett. Show her you love her and propose. She'll be ecstatic."

"No." He wouldn't do that to Eve. She wasn't ready and he might lose her forever if he tried to rush her into marriage.

"Then my money goes to the hideous hyenas." Papa hung up then.

Beck grunted in frustration and shoved his phone in his pocket. Papa was a good man, but it'd always been his way or the highway. Not this time. Beck was going to put Eve first and pray his grandfather would at least be reasonable enough to give his money to a worthy cause. It was out of Beck's hands now. Eve and Paisley were his focus now, even more important to him than hockey. He smiled in the mirror despite the frustrating conversation. He was heading to lunch with them soon and then he and Abbie from the daycare had schemed for him to get a dinner date alone with Eve tonight while Paisley played at Abbie's house. He might finally get that kiss he was craving.

He was happy and in love. He loved his grandfather—the man had been there for Beck throughout every event in his life. Yet if his grandfather couldn't respect his decision to put Eve first, it wasn't Beck's problem.

CHAPTER EIGHT

Eve heard the doorbell as she was strapping on her sandals and her stomach filled with happy bubbles of anticipation. She heard Paisley running for the door and singing, "My Beck, my Beck!"

Eve hurried out of her room and down the steps as Paisley flung the door open. Her song changed to a scream of, "Krew!"

Eve grinned as she reached the foyer and Caleb, Emily, and Krew walked in. Krew and Paisley hugged—it was adorable. Krew towered over Paisley at the very mature age of seven and he was patiently hugging her as if it was his cousinly duty as she clung to him.

Eve hugged Caleb and Emily in turn. They all smiled at their children as Paisley talked a mile a minute to Krew about her "work" and how she was the Ice-skating Princess and her Beck.

Caleb bent down and scooped her up. "Where are my hugs and who is 'my Beck'?"

"That'd be me," a deep voice said from the open doorway.

Caleb whipped around to face Beck. Eve smiled as Beck grinned, tilted his chin to her, and said, "Hello beautiful," and then extended his hand to Caleb. "Beckett Tanner," he said. Whew, just seeing him impressed her, and made her blood run hotter. She wanted to kiss each of his dimples, after she kissed his lips.

"Caleb Jewel." Caleb's response wasn't exactly cold, but he wasn't going to welcome some unknown man into their family circle. He especially would not give any man his blessing to date his little sister, without giving him a hard time.

Paisley leapt from her uncle's arms toward Beck, who caught her easily. "Hi, Princess."

"What is this?" Caleb protested. "I thought you were my girl."

Paisley shrugged adorably and wrapped her arms more tightly around Beck's neck. Eve had seen her little doll in Beck's arms plenty over the past six weeks but she never tired of it. Beck was so strong and tall and Paisley was so cute. Beck was dressed nicer than usual tonight in a white button-down shirt and dark pants. He looked amazing. Luckily she'd opted for a summery, floral dress so she wouldn't feel underdressed next to him.

"Sorry, Uncle Caleb," Paisley said, "but I'm Beck's princess now."

Everyone laughed, but Caleb gave a fake glower. "I am *not* okay with this." He glanced at Eve. "Why haven't we heard a word about Beckett Tanner and somehow Paisley is now his princess?" He said it teasingly but there was a grain of truth that made it hard for Eve to hold Beck's gaze. She talked to her family regularly but she'd avoided their requests to visit, getting pretty creative in her excuses, since she'd been spending every evening with Beck. She hadn't told any of her family members about dating Beck, not even Rachel.

"You stop it, you hear?" Emily pushed at Caleb's shoulder, her beautiful Southern accent giving a lilt to her voice. "Play nice and maybe we'll score tickets to his next game."

"Oh yeah!" Krew cheered. "Be nice, Pops!"

"Next game?" Caleb's brow squiggled.

Emily rolled her dark eyes. She was exquisitely beautiful with her smooth brown skin, black hair, and sparkling eyes. "He's Beckett Tanner. Top defenseman of the Colorado Avalanche."

Caleb stared at his wife. "How do you know that? I thought lacrosse was the only sport you followed."

Eve laughed and Beck grinned at her. "Caleb's a superstar lacrosse hero," Eve explained then blushed as she remembered Paisley had told him that on their first lunch date together.

"I knew that," Beck said. "I've watched some of your games online. Very impressive."

Caleb nodded as if their praise was expected but he grabbed his wife around the waist and pulled her in. "How do you know who Beckett Tanner is? We haven't been to a hockey game."

She gave him a quick kiss and tapped his chest playfully. "Mylee has a poster of him in her workout room."

Caleb finally laughed. "Mylee would."

"Your neighbor?" Eve asked.

"That's the one." Emily grinned. "Bless her heart, she has an obsession with professional athletes. Her poor, poor husband."

Beck was looking a little concerned. Probably wondering if Mylee was a stalker.

"Don't worry," Caleb said. "She's harmless, and she has good taste." He pushed a hand through his hair. "She has multiple posters of me."

Eve and Emily laughed. "Your overconfidence is not winning you any points, mister," Emily said.

"You adore me and you know it." Caleb dipped her and kissed her thoroughly.

"Here they go." Krew rolled his eyes and looked at his younger cousin. "You wanna go to eat at the place where they dive off cliffs?"

"Sure!" Paisley clapped her hands happily.

Caleb finally let Emily up for air and back on her feet. "Let's go, kids," he said. Then he looked at Eve. "We'll give you and Beck some alone time."

Eve's stomach swooped. Though she'd love to be alone with Beck, she didn't know if she was ready. They'd spent time together almost every day for six weeks but Paisley was always there to keep things light. What if he tried to push her for commitment or asked about

Mark or went for a kiss? Her body warmed at the thought of that. Okay, the last one wouldn't be a bad thing, except she hadn't kissed someone in five years. What if she was terrible at it?

"We don't need alone time, we'll come with you," Eve said quickly, too quickly if the deflated look in Beck's eyes was any indicator.

"Yeah," Paisley spoke up. "My Beck and my mama want to come with us."

"I did have reservations at the Capital Grille," Beck said quietly.

"What?" Eve choked. The Capital Grille was very expensive and very high end. "You were planning to take Paisley to the Capital Grille?"

Beck ducked his head. "Abbie offered to babysit."

Conflicting emotions rushed through her: how sweet it was that Beck would want to get her alone and take her to a fancy restaurant but at the same time how presumptuous it was of him to think she'd leave her daughter and be alone with him.

"In my defense," he said softly. "It was Abbie's idea."

Emily was watching them both with slightly arched eyebrows. "Well, I think it's a wonderful idea. But sadly for whoever Abbie is, Caleb, Krew, and I get to spend the evening with Paisley. You'll call and let her know she can have a raincheck?" she asked Beck. He nodded, a sparkle in his blue eyes. Emily took Paisley from Beck's arms and said, "Say goodbye to Beck and Mama, sweet honey child. We'll see them soon."

"Bye, Beck! Bye, Mama," Paisley said.

Eve walked to her daughter and barely got a kiss on the cheek before Emily gave Eve a push toward Beck. She stumbled into Beck's arms and the oxygen seemed to disappear from the room. She couldn't catch a breath but she could smell his yummy cologne and the feel of his muscular body pressed close to hers made her warm and lightheaded.

Beck held her against his chest and smiled. "I like your sister-in-law," he whispered.

Eve couldn't help but let out a giggle Paisley should've claimed.

"What is going on here?" Caleb demanded of his wife. "Did you just push her into his arms?"

"Oh, hush you," Emily shot back at him. "You wouldn't complain about somebody pushing me into your arms." She put one hand on her hip and gave her long hair a sassy toss.

"Yeah, but you're my wife." Caleb jutted out his chin stubbornly. "Eve is my innocent sister."

Eve felt her neck get hot. Her family insisted she was innocent and it seemed that none of her brothers would trust her with a man. She didn't blame them as she'd made the worst choice possible in her first husband.

Emily set Paisley on her feet and sauntered up to her husband, patting him on the cheek. "You've got to let her grow up, love. She can't stay innocent forever."

"I say she can." Caleb's blue eyes flashed.

Eve extracted herself from Beck's arms, her face flaring red. She was the farthest thing from innocent. Did they not realize that she'd been married and had a child? "Okay, Beck and I are going to go now."

Caleb and Emily whipped around to face her and Beck, their feud apparently forgotten. Caleb snaked his arm around Emily's back and Emily blew them a kiss. "Have fun y'all."

"I thought you only blew me kisses," Caleb growled, pulling her in tight against his chest.

"I do a lot more than blow kisses to you," she said back, laughing.

"Oh, my," Eve tried to interrupt their constant flirtations. "Are you actually going to take care of our children?"

Caleb waved her away. "They'll have the best time of their lives." But he didn't seem able to tear his eyes away from his wife.

"We will, Mama," Paisley reassured her.

"Bye, Aunt Eve." Krew waved them off. "I'll take care of Paisley," he said all cute and seven-year-old mature.

Caleb growled something that sounded like, "Later," to Emily. She grinned. He released her and picked up Paisley. "We'll focus on our children one hundred percent."

"Thank you." Beck put his hand on Eve's lower back and escorted her out the door as she gave one last wave to Paisley. He walked her to his fancy car and helped her in. Neither of them said much as they drove into Denver to the restaurant. Eve clasped her hands together and felt nerves assault her. What if they had nothing to say to each other? What if they only worked as a couple when Paisley was around? She loved that Beck was so fabulous with her daughter, but she wanted to have a relationship with just the two of them. Her daughter was her world, but she was aware that sooner than she wanted her little girl would grow up and go out and conquer the world, leaving Eve sadly alone.

CHAPTER NINE

The valet opened Eve's door when they arrived at the restaurant and then took the keys from Beck. His eyes glistened with anticipation as he looked at the car. "Is it really a Bugatti Chiron?" the young man asked. "I'd heard there was one owned by Beckett Tanner but then other people claimed there was only a prototype and the pictures online were doctored."

Beck smiled. "It was specially made." He clapped the young man on the shoulder. "It's okay. It's insured."

The man's eyes bugged out. "Oh, sir, I'll be so careful with it. I see a lot of nice cars, but nothing like..." He trailed off and his jaw went slack. "You *are* Beckett Tanner."

Beck nodded and stuck out his hand. "Nice to meet you..."

"Michael Young," the young man said, obviously in awe and slightly agitated as he shifted his weight quickly from foot to foot.

"Michael," Beck repeated.

Eve noticed as Beck pulled his hand back he had left money in the guy's hand. She loved watching the interaction but snuck a glance for anyone taking pictures.

"Thank you, sir, it's truly an honor." The kid seemed so awestruck,

Eve had to hide a smile. The maître d' was waiting for them to escort them inside and they both gave Michael a quick wave.

They walked into the restaurant and were taken immediately to a private corner table. Eve appreciated Beck's thoughtfulness, as always for not making her be front and center with his superstar status.

Beck pulled out her chair as the maître d' welcomed them. He introduced their waiter who was waiting with bottled water, made some menu recommendations, and took their drink orders before leaving them.

Eve glanced at Beck over the menu. "Do you ever get used to the royalty treatment?"

"It's not about me." He chuckled. "People really like the car."

Eve thought he was more impressive than the car, but obviously the car must be nice from the way that kid had reacted. He'd heard about Beckett's car? Specially made? She didn't think even Joshua and Luke had their cars specially made and they were both billionaires. "Tell me about your car. I'm sadly behind on my fancy car knowledge."

He smiled. "You have knowledge about things much more important than cars."

She laughed.

"There it is. I'd walk across hot lava to earn that laugh." His gaze became a sexy smolder that had her wishing they were completely alone, and not at all worried about if she and Beck worked without Paisley in tow. They would be just fine, more than fine. She suddenly didn't care if she'd forgotten how to kiss. With Beck, a kiss would be incredible no matter what. She knew it.

"The car," she reminded him when she wanted to reach across the table and kiss him.

He leaned back in his chair and started into a story about his grandfather. "My papa's a crusty old guy but... he loves me. He has dozens of cars *almost* as nice as my Bugatti." He winked, obviously proud of his car yet she didn't sense he put much stock in worldly objects. He'd handed the keys to that kid and said "it's insured" as if it wouldn't hurt him if the car got wrecked.

"At every single milestone in my life, Papa would walk me through his glistening shop full of old, restored cars and new, incredible supercars: Bugattis, Maseratis, Lamborghinis, Aston Martins, Rolls Royce, Bentleys."

Her eyes widened as he ticked them off.

"He teased me, tempted me, I was certain that on one of my special days he'd give me one of his prized vehicles—getting my driver's license, as a side note after that memorable walkthrough he had an old, rusted Civic waiting out front for me. Laughed himself silly when he handed me those keys."

Eve laughed. "Oh, my. He sounds like a character."

"You have no idea." He pumped his eyebrows and continued with the list, "Graduating high school, graduating college, getting my master's degree, making my first million on my own investments," Eve found that reassuring, if he was talking about making his first million he wouldn't be after her money. "…being offered the contract with the Avalanche, winning the Stanley Cup," Beck continued. His eyes grew a darker shade of blue and he trailed off for a few seconds before continuing, "It was the day of my parents' funeral that the car that I'd researched and dreamt about for years was delivered to my driveway. My Bugatti Chiron was perfect, even down to the navy blue with silver accents—Papa must've tracked my search history before he had the company custom-make what was only supposed to be a prototype." He toyed with his water glass then took a long swallow. "So now I have a one of a kind vehicle that only means something to me because it's how Papa showed his love. I'd rather have my parents back any day than have that car."

Eve wished she could take his pain away. She put her hand over his. "I'm so sorry, Beck."

He nodded, what else was he supposed to do?

"Thank you for sharing that with me."

The waiter came and took their orders, interrupting the private moment. After the waiter left, the conversation continued with more stories about Beck's parents and grandparents. Eve shared stories too, mostly about her siblings and their growing up years. Beck's grandfather seemed very eccentric and hard-nosed but it was obvious that Beck loved him. Eve was grateful he could share about his parents and appreciated the level of trust that must have taken for him, especially the story about the car.

Their food arrived, but Eve was captivated by Beck's stories and their conversation. She hardly even tasted her filet mignon and veggies. They rarely had time to just talk and she enjoyed each moment of it. After dinner, he took her to the botanical gardens that were luckily quiet tonight as there wasn't a concert or wedding. They held hands as they walked slowly through the dimly lit, lush gardens. They stopped next to a pond and sat on a bench.

Eve's heart was beating faster as she was almost a hundred percent certain he was going to kiss her. He turned to her and gently cupped her cheek with his palm. Studying her, he slowly moved closer. Eve stared into his blue eyes. His warm cologne washed over her. The setting was perfect. This man was perfect, at least to her.

And suddenly, unexpectedly, and against everything she wanted, the doubts and unexplainable fear reared its ugly head. Her chest constricted, her palms grew clammy, and horrible thoughts filled her head. What if Beck was a charming liar like Mark had been? What if Beck, or Mark, weren't the problem at all, but her?

Beck's lips were almost upon hers when she turned her head. His lips brushed her cheek. Several long uncomfortable moments passed, only her labored breathing and the twittering of birds breaking the silence, before he murmured, "Eve?"

She swallowed quick, leaned away, and shook her head. "I'm so sorry, Beck. I'm... not ready."

"Okay." His voice was full of disappointment, but he took a breath and said, "It's okay. We can take it slow." He studied her. "I need to know though... Do you want to date me, Eve? Or have I pushed you too fast, setting up this time to be alone?"

"No! I mean yes. I love being with you. Of course, I want to date you." She blew out a breath of frustration. Why was she acting like this, treating this amazing man like he would hurt her when she knew he was good through and through? "Thank you for taking it slow. You are almost impossible for me to resist." That was too true but obviously didn't explain why she'd just turned her head instead of kissing him.

"Why resist me?" He winked but she could see the vulnerability in his blue eyes. He was as invested as she was in their relationship, in her, and in Paisley. It would hurt him if it didn't work out. Maybe not as much as it hurt her, but she was damaged goods. He was whole and amazing. Despite losing his parents, he was clearly well-adjusted and emotionally stable. She wished she could say the same about herself.

"I'm sorry." She clasped her hands and stared at them. "I've been trying to resist you, having a hard time trusting you, because of my ex." She met his gaze and admitted, "He broke me." That sounded pathetic but it was the truth.

Beck took her hand and murmured, "Can you tell me about it?"

Eve studied him, wondering if he could possibly understand the level of trust she was placing in him sharing this story. Her family obviously knew parts but she hadn't wanted them to know how stupid she'd been and how much Mark had hurt her. She'd tried to act like it was a silly fling or rebellious stage and her beautiful Paisley was all that mattered. Paisley really was all that mattered, but Mark had gouged her from the inside out. He had made her question every unrelated man's intentions since. Could she share everything with Beck? His blue eyes were so sincere and his touch so warm and comforting.

She took a deep breath. If she couldn't trust Beck, they couldn't develop a relationship. For the first time in five years, she wanted a relationship with a man. An amazing man. Beck.

"Mark and I met on the beach of Hilton Head when I was barely graduated from high school. I was on a senior trip with a group of friends. He was charming and he had this ability to get me to spill things I'd never told anyone and make me want to be... more important than I was."

Beck's brow furrowed. "I don't understand what you mean by that. You're the most important person in my world."

Eve gave him a watery smile, willing herself not to cry. "Thank you, Beck." She paused and said, "I guess what I mean is I turned into a bragger of sorts. I let slip how wealthy and accomplished my family was, how we all got a five-million-dollar inheritance, and all the amazing stuff my siblings and parents and I had done." She was the most reserved Jewel sibling. Eve had more in common with her more serious and oldest brother Joshua than her crazy twin brothers, Seth and Caleb. She'd assumed Mark was making her open up and be more outgoing, but he'd been digging information to use to exploit her.

She rolled her eyes and clasped Beck's hand tighter. "Next thing I knew he'd talked me into flying to Vegas and getting married."

Beck's eyebrows dipped. "Without talking to your parents?"

She nodded. "None of my family ever met him."

"What?" Now his eyebrows lifted. It would've been comical if she weren't so humiliated by this conversation and scared to share it.

Eve forced herself to keep talking. "We were married such a short of time, basically just had a three-day honeymoon in Vegas. I thought we'd go visit my family after but when he pried for more details, anxious to get the money rolling in, obviously, I had to explain." She could remember how excited his face had been asking her when the money was coming and then how infuriated he got when she told him the whole truth. "I told him that I had never and would never ask for any help from my parents or my siblings and I received no annuities or monthly checks, and worst of all in his mind, I wouldn't get any inheritance for seven more years. He got mad." Her voice lowered and she swallowed, remembering his rage—kicking furniture, punching walls, screaming at her. "Really mad."

Beck gripped her hand tighter. "Did he touch you?" he asked in a deathly quiet voice.

"No. He kicked and punched inanimate objects and yelled at me, calling me a 'boring stick in the mud'. He said that the only reason any man would marry me was because of my pretty face and my family money. Then he walked out of the hotel room. I never saw him again. I went back to the wedding chapel before I left Vegas and was able to get the marriage annulled." The part she left out was waiting in that hotel room for three long days, praying he'd return. Misery and humiliation like she'd never known when she finally admitted to herself he wasn't coming back and she forced herself to go and annul the marriage. She never would've told her family about any of it if she hadn't later discovered she was expecting Paisley. Her family had of course been too kind and understanding, even with the sparse details she'd shared. She'd never told anyone as much as she was telling Beck. She wondered if he understood the level of trust she was placing in him.

Beck released her hand but gently grasped her shoulders. He turned her to face him and said in a gravelly voice, "You realize he was a liar?"

Eve rolled her eyes. "Well, sure, to trick me into marrying him when he only wanted my money."

"Yes, but also claiming the only reason a man would want to marry you is your pretty face and your family money." His voice deepened. "There are many, many reasons a man would want to marry you."

Eve's stomach swirled with heat, and the fear she usually felt when she even thought of marriage disappeared like a poof of smoke.

"I would want to marry you," Beck said in a sincere tone, "because you're kind, thoughtful, an incredible mother, smart, fun to be around, spiritual, a talented businesswoman, hard-working, committed to family..." His eyes traveled over her. "The fact that your face is the most beautiful face in the world and your body is so gorgeous I have to fight myself not to stare open-mouthed like a hormonal teenager, has very little to do with why I would want to marry you. The fact that your family has money has *nothing* to do with your incredible appeal."

Eve was pulling in quick breaths. She realized Beck wasn't actually proposing but it felt like he was. She wanted to return all of the compliments and more. She never thought she'd find someone so incredible, kind, fun, hard-working, successful, and most important, committed to her and her daughter. The fact that he was irresistibly handsome in every aspect of the word didn't really factor in either. Though it was a nice bonus.

She threw caution to the wind, framed his face with her hands, and pressed her lips to his. The kiss was short but powerful. Eve felt an overwhelming light and joy rush through her.

Beck pulled back and studied her for half a second, searching her gaze, asking if she was ready to commit to him and only him. She nodded in response to his unasked question. Beck grinned, lifted her off the bench and onto his lap, and proceeded to kiss her as if the world was going to end. The kisses were thorough, awe-inspiring, and made her tingle from head to toe. Apparently there was nothing wrong with her kissing ability or maybe the more accurate truth was that her lips and Beck's lips were meant to be locked, creating sweet magic together. Whatever the answer was, she savored each second of the equation and the solution. Beck plus Eve equaled extreme joy.

CHAPTER TEN

Beck went through the next day with the biggest grin on his face. He and Eve had a picnic lunch with Paisley and he stole a quick kiss goodbye when they returned to the gym and Paisley's head was turned.

That night Eve cooked dinner for him and then they went on a walk along the Clear Creek River Trail. He loved doing things with her that many of his friends would think were mundane and boring. He wanted more than anything to be fully invited into she and Paisley's lives. He loved both of them.

Eve had been very cautious before she finally shared with him and then kissed him last night. Each night before she'd said goodbye to him basically on the front porch. Tonight as they returned to her house she said, almost shyly, "Would you like to stay for scriptures and prayers?"

Would he ever? "I'd love to."

They went inside and he waited while she gave Paisley a bath and then his two girls came back down the stairs. Eve gifted him with her beautiful smile and Paisley ran to him, jumping onto his lap. Her hair was wet from her bath and she had on soft pajamas that said Pretty

Princess and had crowns printed all over them. He kissed her forehead, inhaling the sweet scent of baby lotion. "You ready for bed, Princess?"

"No." She put out her bottom lip. "I want to stay up and watch Cinderella with you. But Mama says no." She sighed dramatically. "Well not a hard no, a maybe on the weekend no."

Beck hugged her, grinning. She was so much fun and even more important, Eve was letting him completely into their lives. Forget Papa's billions of dollars, all he needed was these two. Together he and Eve would find other ways to help children throughout the world. He already did with his charity events and bringing kids in need to hockey games and down onto the ice.

"That sounds like a good plan," he said.

"Okay." She pushed out a huffy little breath that made him laugh. "*If* you read me scriptures *and* some Junie B. Jones right now."

"Not so bossy, little miss," Eve said.

"Please," Paisley added.

"I'd love to read to you." Beck gave Eve a smile and held Paisley as they read a few verses of Luke and explained them to Paisley. Then he read a chapter of her silly Junie B. Jones book. Paisley giggled so often he'd pause in his reading to enjoy her laughter and she'd admonish him, "Keep reading."

He caught Eve's tender glance on them as he was reading and lost his place. His mind drifted back to their incredible kisses from last night. Would he receive more tonight? How soon was too soon to beg her to marry him? His need to rush had nothing to do with Papa's inheritance and everything to do with not wanting to walk away from these two, ever. He belonged here, taking care of and loving both of them.

"Beck?" Paisley's sweet voice interrupted his musings. "You stopped reading again."

Beck chuckled and Eve's sweet laughter joined his.

"I think Beck is getting tired." Eve winked at him, letting him know that she didn't believe for one second that he was "tired", and she knew he simply craved more time alone with her. Since she'd trusted him with her story last night, and he'd told her exactly how impressive she was to him, it was like a flood gate of confidence had rushed through her. She'd always seemed competent and confident, but now she glowed. The trust she placed in him made his own chest jut out a little more.

Abbie had promised to take Paisley one night this weekend when Caleb and Emily had trumped her babysitting offer last night. Abbie claimed she owed him for the season tickets and all the paraphernalia he'd given her husband. Beck didn't want anybody owing him anything but he was already planning a date that would be fun and private, ensuring Eve was in his arms most of the night. A hike into the gorgeous mountains east of them where a candlelight dinner would be waiting, then dancing in the moonlit trees, and more kissing than he'd ever experienced.

Beck faked a yawn. Paisley looked disappointed but she perked up when Eve said, "Maybe Beck can carry you up to bed and sing to you."

"Okay!"

Beck stood, swooping Paisley into the air. She giggled and clung to his neck. He waited for Eve to walk in front of them then easily carried Paisley up the stairs, tucked her into bed, and then knelt next to Eve at Paisley's bedside. Their shoulders brushed, and even though he was on his knees, he felt like the king of the rink.

"Would you pray?" Eve asked.

"I would love to." Beck said a short but heartfelt prayer of gratitude for this blessed day, for Paisley, and for Eve, asking a blessing on them and their home.

When he finished, he and Eve stood together.

"Stories of Jesus," Paisley requested.

Beck looked to Eve for help. "I don't know that one."

Paisley stared at him as if he had two heads. "What one *do* you know?"

Beck thought of songs his mom used to sing and grinned. He started to sing in a deep tone, "Oh you can't go to heaven in a limousine, cause the Lord don't sell no gasoline."

Paisley giggled and he continued with the song, the verses out of order but Eve and Paisley's smiles said they didn't care. He got choked up a little bit as he sang, "If you get there before I do, tell my friend I'm coming too." It always made him think of his parents and grandma, especially as his mom had loved this song. Eve's eyes got bright as if she knew exactly what he was feeling. He didn't think she'd lost anyone close to her but she was so compassionate and understanding. He finished with belting out, "I ain't gonna grieve the Lord no more." He thought if he could have Eve and Paisley in his life he'd walk the straight line to heaven without a bit of grief for the good Lord, only praises of gratitude for allowing him the gift of being with these two.

"Kisses," Paisley prompted when he finished.

Eve bent down and kissed Paisley's cheek. "Love you, baby girl."

Beck bent down next and brushed his lips across her forehead. "Goodnight, Princess."

"Love you, Beck!" she sang out happily.

Beck swallowed down the emotion and smiled. "I love you too."

He put his arm around Eve and they walked out into the hallway and then down the stairs. He wanted to sit on the couch and kiss the night away but Eve kept walking toward the front door and he didn't say anything. He understood she still had some reservations about moving too fast and he wouldn't push her, no matter that he could've missed sleep to hold her in his arms all night.

The night air was crisp and cool as only a summer's night in Colorado could be. He inhaled slowly and said, "I love it here."

"In Colorado?" she asked as they stopped on the porch.

"Yes." He glanced down at her. "But mostly here with you and Paisley. Thank you for letting me be part of the nightly routine." His throat got thick and his voice automatically deepened. "Part of your lives."

Eve nodded, biting at her lip as if controlling her own emotions. "Thank you, Beck. I loved hearing you read to her, your prayer, and especially your song." She slid her arms around his neck and Beck's chest swelled as his heart raced faster. "When Paisley said she loved you I thought I'd cry. Thanks for being so wonderful with her."

"She's easy to be wonderful with." Beck bent down closer. "You're even easier to be wonderful with." He smiled. "At least I hope you think I'm 'wonderful' to you also."

She gave him her clear, beautiful laugh and Beck knew he hadn't been this happy since his parents died, or maybe ever.

"I do, Beck."

Beck lit up. He imagined her saying those words so sweetly in front of a preacher. It might have been his grandfather's fault that marriage rested so heavily on his mind, but the more likely instigator of dreams of marital bliss was in his arms. He'd never wanted to be married before and now he couldn't imagine being married to anyone but Eve.

He bent and kissed her, softly at first, but the need for her grew quickly as she let out a sweet whimper of pleasure, dug her fingers into his hair, and pulled him in tighter.

Footsteps approaching on the sidewalk registered somewhere in the back of his mind and then a throat clearing. Beck ignored whoever it was and kept on kissing, but when the throat cleared loudly again he reluctantly pulled back.

Eve gave him a longing look before turning to face whoever was waiting for their attention. Beck caught her lips tightening in disbelief and her blue eyes filling with horror before she whispered, "Mark?"

Beck whipped around to face the man. The weasel had slicked back dirty blond hair, a pretty boy face with pale blue eyes, and a tall, lean build dressed in business casual.

"Eve," the man breathed out, looking up at her on the porch, his eyes raked over her possessively, disgustingly. This man hadn't earned the right to look at his Eve like that.

Beck felt like he was in the hockey rink with his team's honor being threatened if he didn't act. He released Eve, threw down his hands to toss his gloves to the ice, forgetting he didn't have gloves on. Rushing down the steps, he slammed his fist into the man's face. The loser crumpled to the ground, crying out as if Beck had pummeled him with multiple hits, not just one. *Come on.* Beck knew he hit hard, but he would've much preferred the guy trying to fight back so he could hit him some more. This jerk had hurt Eve deeply and he deserved pain, lots of it.

Beck stood over him, waiting for the guy to straighten or get mad and fight or something. Mark simply stayed on his knees, clutching his face, and moaning in pain.

Beck looked to Eve for guidance. She stood on the porch, white-faced, not moving. He didn't know if she was upset he'd hit the guy or upset the guy had shown up here. Beck decided it was the latter and bent down low. "You are not welcome here. If you ever try to hurt Eve again I'll hurt you much, much worse than a simple jab to the face. Get out of here... now."

The guy finally scrambled to his feet, clutching his hand to his eye as if Beck had poked it out with a hot poker. "I'll sue you," he threatened in a whiny voice.

Beck chuckled darkly. "You're trespassing on private property and I don't think you want the wrath of the Jewel or the Tanner families coming down on your scrawny neck for how you've treated Eve. Get out of here."

Eve had said her family never even met this loser. He could imagine how Caleb would react to the guy. Beck raised a threatening fist, knowing he'd have Caleb's support. "*Don't* make me ask again," he growled low and threatening.

The guy's eyes widened, he cast one more glance at Eve, turned, and ran for the silver Lexus parked at the curb. Beck turned back to Eve. His brow wrinkled with concern. "Are you okay?"

She gave a little whimper, darted down the stairs, and threw herself against his chest. Beck caught her easily and held her as silent tears streamed down her smooth cheeks. He stroked her hair and whispered what he hoped were comforting words. "It's okay. I've got you. He's gone," over and over again. He was relieved that she'd run to him and wasn't mad about him getting physical and punching the guy, but he was very concerned that simply seeing that loser had this effect on her.

Finally, Eve pulled back and dashed away the moisture from her face with the back of her hand. "Sorry. I don't want you to think I care about him, at all. It was simply the shock of seeing him and..." She reached up and kissed him, she tasted of salt and his dreams of happiness. "Thank you. Seeing you punch him was the best thing ever." She tilted her head. "Well, not the absolute best. Seeing you with Paisley in your arms is the absolute best thing I've ever seen."

Happiness rushed through him and the love he felt for her could not be contained. He tugged her in close and proceeded to kiss her until they were both gasping for air. Resting his forehead against hers, he said, "Seeing you smile... that's the best thing I've ever seen. Hearing you laugh... that's the best thing I've ever heard. Holding you close... that's the best thing I've ever felt."

She smiled tremulously.

"I love you, Eve." He felt it clear through and hoped she knew how sincere he was.

"I love you, Beck."

The emotion rising in his throat would have been humiliating in any other circumstance. Beck didn't care. He loved her so much he would grind all his man cards into the ice in front of his teammates if that's what it took to show her what she meant to him. Luckily, she went onto her tiptoes and kissed him, distracting him before he did lose those man cards by tearing up or breaking down completely. He hadn't felt pure, sincere love since his parents had died. He returned her kisses and then some, filled to bursting with love and happiness. Eve and Paisley were his—his future, his love, his happiness. Nothing would take them away from him.

CHAPTER ELEVEN

Eve finally forced herself to give Beck one last kiss and head into her house. She should've been terrified that Mark had reappeared in her life, but with Beck around what was there to worry about? She was proud of her own reaction to Mark. She'd been a mess for a few seconds, but Beck had quickly helped her see what a pathetic loser her ex was. It felt as if Mark had no hold over her anymore and she could soar with Beck holding her hand.

She hummed Beck's silly song about not riding roller skates to heaven as she got ready for bed. She was scrubbing her teeth with vigor and bent down to spit. Rising up with a smile, she gasped when she saw a dark shadow out in her bedroom.

Dropping her toothbrush, she whirled around, trying desperately to remember where her cell phone was. In her purse? On the dresser? Had Paisley been playing with it earlier? She had to call for help. Beck! He'd save her, but he was probably home in bed already.

The shadow approached and if she were alone she would've slammed the door but Paisley was out there. She stood up straighter. She was strong and she would fight to protect her daughter.

"Eve," the man said softly, finally revealing his face in the light from the bathroom. His eye and cheek were red from Beck hitting him.

"Mark." Eve didn't know if she was relieved it wasn't some random intruder, or more terrified that it was Mark. Yet even when he was angry enough to punch holes in the wall of their hotel room he'd never hurt her. That was at least some reassurance. "What are you doing? How did you get in?"

"Remember how you told me the code you and your family all use? Your dad's birth month and year. 0858."

Eve was disgusted with herself, thinking about all the things she'd told him. As she looked into his pale blue eyes she couldn't believe she'd been so naïve as to trust him. She could see in his countenance—it was obvious to her now that she had some world experience and her testimony was deeper and brighter—Mark was dark and evil. How had she not seen it? She tried to give herself some slack. She'd been eighteen and never felt love and flattery like his before. She knew she shouldn't be so hard on herself, but she was. Where was her phone so she could call Beck? She'd love to see him knock Mark to the ground again.

She edged out of her bathroom, walked across her bedroom, and flipped on the light, looking around for her phone. "What are you doing here, Mark?"

He splayed his hands and put a simpering expression on his face. "I've ached for you all these years, Eve. When I saw all the media about Rachel being burned and then Caleb being framed for murder, I kept trying to put you from my mind but I couldn't do it any longer. So I tracked you down."

"I want nothing to do with you."

Mark took a few steps closer. She held up a hand and he stopped.

"Please, Eve. We were young and I made so many mistakes. You have to know that you were my first love and as the years have passed I realize that you're my only true love. No woman can compare to you."

"What do you want now, Mark? I still don't have my inheritance."

She gave him a fierce glower that would've had even her brothers backing up.

He did back a step but he looked imploringly at her. "It was never about your money, love."

She harrumphed in disgust. "Save it, Mark."

"It wasn't." He stepped forward again. "I didn't feel worthy of you. I was mad at myself for not being enough for you. I wanted to earn my way, make something of myself, and then I knew I'd be worthy of you. I'm a successful accountant in Savannah now. I can provide well for us." He glanced around. "Not that you aren't doing well for yourself, this is a beautiful house. You're not... married to that guy?"

"Not yet." She raised her eyebrows imperiously. She and Beck were nowhere near being engaged but they'd both said they loved each other tonight. "I don't want anything you have to offer, Mark. You need to leave." It was amazing how he could try to twist what happened between them. What a narcissistic liar.

She started toward her bedroom door, praying he'd follow. He did, but he moved quicker than she'd expected, catching her in the hall and grabbing her elbow. "Eve, please." He stared into her eyes, probably assuming it was a beseeching look but all it said to her was: "I'm a politician who would lie to his own mother to get what I want, stab her in the back, and do it all with a smile on my face."

"My Beck," a sleepy murmur came from just down the hall. "Mama."

Eve's heart slammed against her chest, but her body felt frozen. "Paisley," she murmured. Breaking from Mark, she hurried to her daughter's room and looked in the open doorway. Paisley was still in bed and looked to be asleep. She'd probably been dreaming.

Mark crowded in behind her and stared at their daughter sleeping in her princess room. Eve hated how he tainted this room. This was her and Paisley's house, their sanctuary. He had not right to be here.

She whirled to face him. "You need to leave."

He was staring at Paisley, wide-eyed and open-mouthed. "She's mine," he said simply.

"No, she's not," Eve insisted.

Mark looked back and forth between Eve and Paisley for a few seconds and then he moved quickly. He grabbed her by the shoulders, pulled her into the hallway, and pushed her against the wall. Eve's breath rushed out and her heart picked up again. He stared into her eyes and she tried for a poker face, praying he wouldn't see the truth.

"She's mine," he repeated with a glower of triumph in his eyes. His red eye and cheek would've been almost comical if she weren't so upset. "I have a daughter."

"She's not your daughter," she reasserted.

"Oh, yes she is." His eyes turned mean and cold. "You stole her from me. All these years. I should've known. I should've been with her."

Eve couldn't take anymore. "You deserted me when I was expecting her," she said through clenched teeth. "You are not on the birth certificate and you have no rights. You try to come near her and I will have you arrested. I'll be filling out a restraining order in the morning and changing the codes on my doors. Leave… now."

Mark actually released her and stepped back. His eyes were wide with surprise. Eve had never been so calm and focused as she was right now. She'd never really stood up to anyone, even when she turned men down for dates she always used some excuse. Her brothers had always watched out for her with their brawn and Rachel had protected her with her sharp tongue. She adored her siblings, but it felt good to stand up for herself.

Mark looked her over as if gauging how serious she was.

"Right now," she said even more firmly, pointing for the staircase.

Mark backed up and said, "This isn't over, Eve. You hid her from me and I have rights."

"No, you don't." She folded her arms across her chest and stood straighter. She was a fitness pro and a mama bear and he was a slimy wimp. She could take him out any time she wanted. "And unless you'd like to be arrested, or get punched in the face by me, and by my stud of a boyfriend again, dang that was fun to watch, I suggest you go back to Savannah and keep Colorado on your do not travel list."

Mark visibly swallowed and then turned to scuttle down the stairs. He was obviously afraid of Beck but he also seemed afraid of Eve. She followed him down the stairs, waited for him to exit the front door, and then turned the deadbolt. She wanted to call Beck or one of her siblings but instead, she found her phone, in the living room couch cushions where Paisley must've been playing with it, and called a twenty-four-hour locksmith. The codes on the doors were getting changed tonight.

Eve had taken care of herself and Paisley for the past five years, but she didn't know that she'd ever felt so brave and strong. She smiled as she thought of Beck. He'd given her strength. He loved her. Mark couldn't hurt her ever again.

CHAPTER TWELVE

Eve woke early the next morning even though she'd been up late waiting for the locksmith to finish and then had a hard time settling down, checking on Paisley and kissing her cheek and forehead repeatedly throughout the night. She did a weight workout in her exercise room, showered, and made Paisley pancakes for breakfast.

Her darling girl skipped down to the table in her princess nightgown. "Cake-cakes! I love you, Mama!"

Eve hugged her tightly. "I love you too, doll."

They headed to the gym after Paisley ate and got ready. Eve felt a dart of trepidation as she dropped her girl off at the daycare. She knew she was being silly but something had her unsettled. Mark wasn't stupid enough to kidnap Paisley, right? He could try to prove paternal rights but that would take time and money. She doubted he cared about her or Paisley unless he thought they could bring him money. He was probably long gone.

She met with her first training appointment, Trudy, but noticed the second Beck walked into the gym. Her face lit up with a happy smile. He caught her eye and returned her grin. Eve wanted to be alone with him and tell him everything that had happened with Mark. She knew he'd be proud of her for being so strong and she could hardly wait to kiss him and hear him say he loved her again. She wondered if she should've called him last night or this morning. Would he be upset that she hadn't? She wasn't very good at this dating stuff but she felt certain Beck wouldn't get upset with her. She also knew he'd protect her, trust her, be there for her, kiss her until she wanted to beg him to marry her. Her stomach swooped. Where had that last thought come from? Maybe someday she and Beck could talk marriage, but it was definitely a long, long way off.

"Somebody is whipped," Trudy said, grunting through a clean and press.

"Oh, yes, I am," Eve admitted.

"Ooh-ee." Trudy set the weighted bar down and wiped her forehead with a chilled towel. "You are the luckiest woman in Colorado."

"Maybe in the nation," Eve said, winking. She caught Beck's gaze again and felt her cheeks go red. Had he heard her? She'd tell him that herself, she'd yell it to the world.

She forced Trudy back to work. The time went slowly as she trained Trudy until ten then a young mom named Lolly until eleven. Beck caught her eye often and sent the most appealing smiles in her direction. John was her eleven o'clock appointment and the man acted really strange. He was irritable and seemed like he wanted to tell her something but then he'd clamp his lips shut and push through a lift with a huffy breath. Every time he caught her gazing at Beck he'd mutter something indiscernible.

Finally, Eve asked, "Is everything okay, John? You seem… off."

He set down his weights and stared at her. "Are you dating Beckett Tanner?"

She smiled and nodded. "Yes, I am."

"Are you going to marry him?" he demanded.

Eve stepped back. "We just started dating. It's not that serious, as in marriage serious." She felt guilty the instant she said that. It was serious. They'd told each other they loved each other. Yet she was pretty marriage-phobic after Mark. But she also knew Beck was nothing like her ex and she was grateful he was willing to take it slow for her.

John seemed to settle down. "Oh, okay. I don't want to badmouth anyone, but if it gets serious... please talk to me before you commit to anything." He cast another glare Beck's way.

Eve wondered if he was just jealous because she'd turned him down for several date offers. She couldn't imagine anything he could say that would not cast Beck in a positive light. She was grateful when they finished and John went on his way.

She hurried to her office to put on lip gloss and spritz on some body splash then speed-walked back down the stairs and toward the daycare. Beck was already there, holding Paisley as she talked a mile a minute. Abbie stood nearby. They all glanced her way as she approached and Eve loved Paisley's happy cry of, "Mama!" and she loved Beck's warm, appreciative glance. Seeing her girl in this strong, incredible man's arms was perfect. It felt so right. He felt so right.

Beck walked to her and stole a quick kiss. "Lunch?"

She nodded. "Can we get takeout from D'Deli and go to the park?" It was actually Eve's turn to provide lunch and she usually made a picnic but she had been tired and off this morning. She knew Beck wouldn't care what they ate, as long as they were together.

"The park?" Paisley clapped her hands. "That's my bestestest place!"

They shared a smile, thanked Abbie, and headed outside. They grabbed lunch and found a spot at a picnic table close to the playset where they could watch Paisley play and still talk.

The story of Mark coming back last night spilled out quickly. Beck was furious at Mark but reassured Eve she'd done exactly what she should've done. They forgot all pretense of eating as Beck pulled her in close and kissed her forehead. "I'm so proud of you. You're such a strong, brave woman."

Eve cuddled into him. "Thank you."

"Next time... please call me so I can hit him again?"

Eve laughed. "There won't be a next time, sorry." She smiled up into his blue eyes and cupped his cheek with her palm. "Have I told you that I love your eyes?"

He gave her a smoldering look with those eyes. "Not as much as I love yours."

"Have I told you I love your lips?" She stole a quick kiss.

"Not as much as I love yours." He kissed her longer.

"Have I told you how much I love your beard?"

"Not as much as..." He trailed off and then laughed, revealing the dimples she loved underneath that beard. "You got me."

Eve pushed at his chest with her free hand. "Your compliments were completely insincere. You were just parroting."

He bent down close. "I'll show you what's sincere." Then he was kissing her and she wasn't going to stop that to tease him.

They smiled at each other as they pulled apart and both instinctively turned to look for Paisley. Eve's gaze swept over the large playground, searching for the dark hair and the pink t-shirt. "Do you see her?" she asked Beck, not really concerned. There were so many tunnels and tube slides and playground objects to hide behind.

"No." He stood and said, "I'll take the right side."

Eve loved him so much. Paisley was going to tumble out of a slide any second or they'd hear her happy voice talking with another child, but Eve loved that Beck took watching her little girl seriously as she also stood and started skirting the playground to the left.

Eve carefully looked inside the slides and tubes and behind the obstacles. That flash of pink shirt and contrasting dark hair wasn't appearing. Her stomach started feeling a little squeamish and her gaze darted over to the river. Clear Creek was a lot tamer this late in the summer, without the spring runoff, and Paisley loved going to one of the many areas where manmade steps went down into the water, but she wouldn't go on her own. Eve had warned her far too many times.

Beck met up with her and shook his head tightly. They both looked to the river and Eve's stomach plunged. "She wouldn't, would she?" Beck asked.

Eve shook her head. "I don't think so. I've drilled it into her head that she can't go there without me."

She heard a light laughter and her head darted up. Disappointment slithered through her as she saw it was a little blonde girl in a blue shirt. Yet she'd noticed minutes ago that Paisley was playing some chase game with that girl and her blond brother who looked to be a couple years older. She hurried over to them. "Were you playing with Paisley?" She tried to smile encouragingly so as not to scare them.

"Yeah," the little boy said. "We were playing hide and seek in the tubes and slides but then she went with her dad that way." He pointed to the west across the park. There was a community center there and a parking lot adjacent to it. She couldn't see Paisley or some man this kid thought was her dad.

"Her dad?" Her stomach felt like it would fall out. Her dad? She looked up at Beck for help.

"Did he have blond hair, looked like a weasel?" Beck asked the kid.

The little boy shrugged in confusion.

"Yellow hair?" Eve clarified.

"Yep."

Beck took off at a sprint over the playground and across the grass. Eve followed, panic making her breath come so fast she felt light-headed and dizzy as she ran.

"No!" Beck roared as they approached the parking lot and a silver Lexus pulled out, heading north. Beck sprinted after them but the car sped up.

"Please no, please no," Eve screamed out in anguish. Her baby girl. Her daughter. The light of her life. Gone. Had Beck gotten the license plate? What could they do to find her? She dialed 911, knowing the police were their only hope now but the terror of Paisley being gone with Mark consumed her.

Beck was still chasing the car but it was growing farther away. Eve wanted to collapse and sob, but she had to stay focused and do all she could to help the police find Paisley. She prayed desperately in her heart. She knew she couldn't survive without her little girl.

CHAPTER THIRTEEN

Eve was certain her world had collapsed. Her legs barely supported her as she tried to think logically. The phone rang twice and an eternity seemed to pass before the call connected.

"911, what's your emergency?" the operator said.

"My girl... kidnapped," she got out. A flash of movement to her left caught her eye. Was that a pink shirt and dark hair?

She whirled and saw Mark scurry from behind a huge tree trunk, carrying Paisley the other direction toward the visitor's center. Beck had chased after the silver car and was too far away to help.

"Stop!" Eve screamed. "Mark!" She ran their direction. Mark cast a glance over his shoulder and upped his pace. Even though Paisley was still in danger, the sight of her gave Eve hope. At least she wasn't speeding toward the unknown in a silver Lexus.

"Mama!" Paisley cried out, wriggling to be free of Mark's arms.

Eve ran faster than she'd ever run, gripping her phone with slick fingers. She'd talk to the dispatcher after she caught Mark and hit him harder than Beck had last night. How dare he steal her daughter?

Mark skirted behind the building. Did he have another car there? Had that even been his car that had disappeared? Was Beck still chasing that car? She didn't have time to look for Beck as she made it around the side of the building. Some overgrown bushes snagged on her shirt and tugged at her. Eve pushed on, yelling for Paisley.

She tripped over something and went sprawling. She heard Paisley crying for her and tried to scramble to her feet. A whoosh of sound had her glancing to the side. She saw Mark chuck a log at her forehead. Eve went down hard, pain shooting from her head. The world around her swirled and all she could see for a moment was black. The pain was so intense she feared she'd vomit.

"Mama!" Paisley screamed.

"You hid her from me for five years," Mark yelled at her. "Now you're going to have to pay to get her back!"

Eve struggled to her knees, everything was spinning. She could hear Paisley's cries growing fainter, but she couldn't get to her feet. It hurt too much. No! She couldn't let her daughter down.

"Eve!" Beck wrapped his arm around her and lifted her to her feet. He was here. Her hero. Her protector. He'd save Paisley.

She was so dizzy, she leaned heavily against him, but she couldn't afford to be weak. "Paisley," she begged him, pulling away and leaning against the building. "Save her."

Beck released her and took off. Eve's vision cleared and she saw Beck hurtling after Mark and Paisley. She forced herself to cling to the building and shuffle after them. She'd lost her phone somewhere. Would any other help come? Hadn't anyone at the park seen Mark kidnap her daughter?

She came around the rear of the building and a small parking lot in time to see Mark shove Paisley into a black SUV through the driver's side door and try to jump in himself.

Beck reached him, grabbed his arm, and yanked him back out. Eve kept moving forward. She had to get to her girl. Mark screamed in horror as Beck slammed his fists into the jerk's face and body. Mark kept knocking back into the car and bouncing back into another hit from Beck. Mark slid to the ground and put his arms over his head. "Stop! I'll leave them alone!"

Sirens cut through the air and people appeared around the building. Eve glanced over as a mom, holding the blonde girl in the blue shirt told her. "We called the police. Are you okay?"

Eve nodded her head. It hurt. She wasn't okay but Paisley was and that was all that mattered. "Thank you," she managed.

Beck stepped over Mark, growling, "Stay down."

Mark looked up at him and just whimpered.

Paisley scrambled out of the vehicle and into Beck's arms. "My Beck, my Beck," she cried over and over again.

Eve found renewed energy as she straightened and walked a wobbly line to the two people who meant everything to her. Paisley was clinging to Beck's neck and he was patting her back and saying something to her. He saw Eve and his eyes widened. He rushed her way.

"Eve!"

She held up a hand, wondering how bad she looked. At least there wasn't any blood but she was sure she'd have bruises. "I'm okay," she murmured.

Beck jogged to her. He pulled her in close and she laid against his strong chest, encircling one arm around his back and wrapping her other arm around Paisley.

"Mama," Paisley cried. "You okay?"

"I'm okay, sweet girl. Are you okay?"

"He said he was my daddy and wanted to give me a present. Then he tried to steal me."

"The scum," Beck growled.

Eve's head had been clearing and the pain calming but the anger at Mark made the ache rear again. How dare he? She forced herself to just hold on to Beck and Paisley, instead of going to kick the loser while he lay there like the wuss he was.

"Thank you for saving me, my Beck," Paisley said.

Tears slid down Eve's face. Beck's strength was holding her up now and he had just rescued her daughter. "Yes, thank you," she managed.

"I love you, Pais," Beck said. "I will always watch out for you."

"I love you," Paisley said loudly, smacking his cheek with her lips.

Eve's heart swelled in her as she glanced up at the two of them.

Beck gently kissed the side of her forehead that wasn't throbbing. "I love you," he murmured.

"I love you. Thank you, Beck." She needed to gush out her gratitude but that was enough for now. Tonight she'd show him exactly how much she appreciated him.

They clung to each other in their little circle as more people arrived to gawk and then police cars flooded the scene and uniformed officers started to sort out the mess. Eve was so relieved and so in love with Beck. She owed him everything, and never wanted to let him go.

Beck waited very impatiently after the EMTs cleared Eve and then the police had to separate them for questioning. He only knew he had to have Eve and Paisley back in his arms. He didn't think that he'd ever forget the terror he felt after realizing Eve's psychotic ex had stolen their girl. Their girl. Beck and Eve's girl. It was true. No matter what, he had to be with Eve and Paisley. They were his and they all belonged together. Now to convince Eve of that.

The police finally released them. One of the officers came in and explained that Mark had confessed to kidnapping Paisley hoping for a ransom from Eve's family. They also found the silver Lexus Mark had rented. He'd paid a seventeen-year-old to drive away on his signal as a distraction. Beck was grateful the guy's plan hadn't worked. He couldn't stand the thought of Paisley scared and confused without her mom or Beck.

The police took them back to the gym to get their cars, Beck caught a glimpse of Eve staring longingly at him. He thought it might not be too difficult to convince her that they all belonged together. They drove together in his Bugatti to Eve's house. They'd get her car tomorrow. He would sleep on the couch. He wasn't going to leave them, not tonight, not ever.

It was early evening when they walked tiredly inside. Beck turned to Eve and she did exactly what he'd hoped. She flung herself at him and held on tight. Paisley wasn't about to be left out as she said, "Hold me, my Beck."

Beck grinned, swooped the little girl up, and easily held her in the crook of his right arm as he held Eve close with his left. When Eve pulled back, rather than confess his undying love and his desires to marry her and adopt Paisley he said, "Do you want to take a bath and Paisley and I will order takeout and find a movie to watch?"

"Do I stink?" she teased with a sweet smile on her lips.

Beck chuckled, grateful she could tease after what they'd been through. "You smell delectable," he smiled, "I just thought you might want to relax. That was quite a hit you took to the head."

"Nowhere near as hard as the hits you gave Mark." Her voice sounded thick with emotion. "Thank you, Beck. Thank you so much."

Beck searched her blue gaze. Maybe it was time. "I will always be there for you, Eve."

She smiled tremulously and her eyes brightened before tears spilled over her dark lashes. Beck's stomach plummeted.

"Why you making my mama cry?" Paisley demanded.

"I didn't mean to," Beck rushed to say.

Eve held up a hand. "No, these are good tears. I love you, Beck." Her voice got low and fierce. "You promise you'll never leave us?"

"Never." He swallowed hard and said in what he hoped was a level tone because he was so full of love for her and Paisley that he was afraid his voice would crack. "Marry me, Eve, please."

Her eyes widened and her mouth formed the prettiest little bow.

"I know it's quick and I know it's crazy, but I want to be with you two. Always. I can't stand one more day without knowing you're mine, one more night without you sleeping next to me." The words were so sappy his teammates would've died laughing but he'd say sappier ones if it would convince Eve of his sincerity. "Please, marry me."

Eve bit at her lip. Her gaze darted to Paisley and lingered there as if trying to decide what was the best thing for her daughter. He wanted to reassure her that he would love and provide for both of them, raise

Paisley as his own, he already felt like he loved her like a father, but he forced himself to wait. The moments passed and he didn't know how long he could stand the wait. He loved Eve completely and couldn't imagine ever wanting to be apart.

She finally met his gaze. Her blue eyes were warm, lit up, and so inviting it was all he could do to not kiss her and then ask the question again.

"Yes," she said, breathlessly, beautifully. "Of course, I'll marry you, yes!" She wrapped her arms around his neck and kissed him until Paisley pushed her face against Beck's cheek.

"Stop," Paisley begged.

Beck chuckled. "Sorry, Pais." He wanted to kiss Eve for a long, long time but luckily Paisley went to bed around eight-thirty. He could control himself until then. He did have to ask though, staring deeply into Eve's eyes. "Soon?"

Eve laughed and that glorious sound filled him up. "Tomorrow?" she said.

Beck's insides overflowed with a warmth that was partially the physical desire Eve stirred in him, but mostly the desire to be the man worthy of her. She loved him and she wanted to marry him tomorrow? He could hardly believe it. Especially as he'd sensed many times that she needed to go slow, learn to trust him, and really know he would be there for her. "Are you serious?"

She laughed again. "No."

He felt the letdown but it was okay. He could be patient, for Eve. He could wait a year if she wanted to plan some fancy, huge wedding. He'd hate it, but he could wait.

"Isaac's not in the country," she said. "Some secret Special Ops mission."

She wanted her family there, of course, she did. "It's fine, love. We can wait as long as you need."

She gave him a mischievous grin that filled him with happiness. "But I'm pretty sure he's got time off next weekend. What do you think of August sixteenth for a wedding date? That's Saturday, right?"

The warmth that rushed over Beck now was close to an explosion. She trusted him, she would get married quickly, for him. It was a better gift than any present he'd ever received on August sixteenth. "That's my birthday."

"Oh. No." Her mouth pursed and he got distracted for a second, wanting to kiss her. "That won't work."

"Yes, it will. You and Paisley will be the best birthday present in the world."

It hit him like an unseen sucker punch that he would also get his inheritance and be able to give it to children throughout the world. He'd have to tell Eve all about that. He looked into her blue, glistening eyes. Tomorrow. They were both emotionally drained right now. Tonight they'd eat takeout, snuggle and watch a movie, and then kiss the night away after Paisley fell asleep. Tomorrow was soon enough to tell her he'd inherit billions on their wedding day. He knew she wouldn't care about the money and would agree to use it for charitable purposes. She was so perfect for him.

"August sixteenth then," she said.

She leaned closer and Beck wasted no time kissing those tempting lips until Paisley pushed in close. "'That'll do, son, that'll do'," she said in the imitation of some movie he couldn't think of right now.

Beck and Eve pulled apart and both laughed. "All right little Princess," he smiled down at Paisley, "What kind of takeout should we order?"

She wrinkled her nose. "McDonald's!"

He and Eve shared a glance. "Try again," Eve said.

"Ah, crap. How's about pizza? And a salad for Mama?"

"Better."

Beck carried Paisley to the couch and they all settled in together. Together. That was all he wanted. Together with his girls.

CHAPTER FOURTEEN

The next morning at the gym Eve felt like she was floating. She and Beck were going to go shop for engagement rings after he practiced at the rink and she finished work this afternoon. Then they'd FaceTime each of her family members, starting with her dad for Beck to ask for her hand, and then his grandfather. She'd let Rachel plan the wedding. Her sister would love that.

Beck texted her this morning that he had some big news to share over dinner. Abbie had volunteered to watch Paisley since Beck had some extravagant date planned. Eve assumed he'd formally ask her to marry him tonight in some romantic setting once they had the ring.

She had a nine o'clock training with an older lady named Isabel. John stalked over to her the moment she finished at ten o'clock and hissed, "I need to talk to you in your office."

She blinked up at him. "Something wrong with the gym or your training?"

"You could say that."

She swallowed and walked with him to the stairs that led to her office. She didn't need him to attack her gym or her training in front of everyone. Beck watched her walk away and gave her a questioning glance but she smiled at him and gave him an ok symbol to let him know all was well.

Eve walked into her office, followed by John. He sat heavily in the chair in front of the desk. She didn't shut the door. Not that she didn't trust him but it was just safer that way. Hopefully, he wasn't too upset and wouldn't start yelling. John didn't seem like that type though.

"What's going on, John?" she asked.

"You might want to sit down," he said quietly.

She arched her eyebrows and didn't comply. "I'm fine standing." Looking at him, she nodded her encouragement. Whatever it was he might as well get it out.

"You're marrying Beckett Tanner," he stated.

"Yes," she said. "How'd you hear?"

"Trudy."

She suddenly remembered John asking her if it was serious with Beck and she'd said no. He'd asked her to talk to him before she committed to Beck. She hadn't even thought of his request again until this moment. Yet what business was it of John's anyway?

He pushed out a heavy breath. "I was in the locker room not long ago and overheard Beckett talking to someone. He called him Papa."

Eve nodded. "His grandfather." Her gut churned and she had no clue why.

"There's no easy way to say this," John clenched his hands and then rushed out. "He's marrying you for money, Eve."

"Excuse me?" Beck had plenty of his own money. He didn't need to marry her for her inheritance. He wasn't like Mark. Fear pricked at her spine but she refused to believe it. No way. Beck was nothing like Mark.

"Not your money. His grandfather's. The guy seemed to be threatening him. If Beckett doesn't get married by a certain date, I gathered it was soon, his grandfather will gift his billions to someone else."

Eve's legs weakened. She stumbled over to her desk chair. John sprang to his feet and helped her sit down. "No," she whispered. Not Beck. He'd been so patient with her, so committed to her and Paisley, so perfect. Would he truly marry her to get billions of dollars? That was an insane amount of money. Who wouldn't be swayed by that much money?

"I'm sorry," John said. "I wouldn't want you to be hurt, but I didn't want you to marry someone under false pretenses and for all the wrong reasons."

False pretenses. Lies. The wrong reasons. She'd wanted to marry Beck for all the right reasons. She thought. She loved him. She'd grown to trust him completely. He adored her daughter and had saved Paisley from Mark. Beck was good, kind, fun, spiritual, talented, amazing in every which way... and he'd lied to her. Maybe it wasn't as bad as she feared. John could have misunderstood the conversation. Sadly, it didn't matter. If there was any truth to Beck marrying her for money it would hurt her far worse than Mark ever did.

She sat there in a stupor trying to think it all through. Was Beck like Mark? He cared for her. He obviously loved Paisley. Did he love Eve? Did he love her enough? Was she simply the best option so he could get his money? No wonder he'd asked her to marry him so quickly and when she was emotionally a mess after the kidnapping attempt. That had been a smart move on his part. She'd trusted him so deeply and would've said yes to anything he'd asked yesterday.

Her head ached as if Mark had slammed another log into it. Was Beck planning to stay with them after he got his billions or ditch them? She wished she knew the stipulations of his grandfather's will. Would they have to stay married for a certain length of time? Maybe she could make him fall in love with her in whatever time she got with him. Somehow convince him she was worthy of him and he wouldn't leave her sitting alone in a hotel room, watching the door—desperate, alone, heartbroken.

Her spine straightened and horror rushed through her. No. She wasn't going to grovel for Beck's affections like she sadly would've for Mark's years ago. She'd never forget waiting in that hotel room for days, ordering takeout, and trying to distract herself with books, games on her phone, and movies, jumping each time she heard movement in the hallway. She hadn't dared leave in case Mark changed his mind and came for her. She would *never* act so needy and desperate again. Not even for Beck who she loved desperately compared to the lame fake love she'd had for Mark.

Glancing around she realized John was gone. She tried to take some steadying breaths. She closed her eyes and said a prayer. She would've called Rachel for advice but there was a soft rap on the doorframe and there he stood. Beck. He was glorious. He was glistening with sweat from his workout and his muscles popped in his arms. His handsome face and bright blue eyes were more serious than usual. No dimples showed through his trimmed beard. Was he concerned for her, or for what she may have heard?

"You okay?" he asked.

Eve bit at her lip, willing herself not to cry. She shook her head.

Beck hurried into the room and knelt next to where she sat. The move made her want to cry even more. He appeared so genuine, so invested in her, so patient and exactly what she and Paisley needed. He took both her hands in his and said, "I'd hug you but I'm all sweaty."

Eve forced a smile. It was good he thought he stunk because if he held her right now she'd fall apart.

"What's going on?" he asked, his blue eyes earnest. "Something else with Mark?"

"No." A tear spilled over and she hurriedly brushed it away.

"What happened, love? What did John do?"

Eve had to get this out. She pulled her hands free and stood, walking around her chair and against the wall to create some distance between them. Beck stood and he looked even more incredible. Were his insides as perfect as his outsides like she'd come to believe or had she been duped again? Anger rose inside her. She was done being the trusting weakling. She was strong—raising her daughter on her own, putting herself through school, buying the gym, standing up to Mark. She could do this.

"I just have one question," she said slowly and carefully.

"Ask me anything," Beck said, but there was concern in his eyes now. Not just concern for her, but concern for what she would ask.

"If you are married by... your birthday." It came to her even though she wasn't certain that was true. "Will you inherit billions?"

The instant alarm and distress in Beck's eyes was all the confirmation she needed. He held up his hands. "Listen, Eve. I was going to tell you."

"Oh, you were? When? On our honeymoon?" The horror of that fear choked her. Mark had ditched her on their honeymoon. Would Beck have done the same? She put a hand to her throat.

"No. Tonight. You remember how I said I had something big to share with you?" He forced a smile. "Surprise."

Eve's eyes widened and a fury stronger than what she'd felt toward Mark surfaced. She stomped toward Beck and poked him in the chest. "At least Mark came clean eventually. You just planned on keeping on lying to me, didn't you?"

Beck's blue gaze filled with anger as well. "Never compare me to that scum-ball. I would never hurt you like that. I love you. I love Paisley."

Eve didn't want to hear about his love. "If you loved me, you would've told me the truth."

"I am telling you the truth. It's not about the money."

Eve glared at him. "Keep telling yourself that, maybe someday you'll believe it, but I never will." Grabbing her purse off her desk, she stomped around him, half expecting and hoping for him to grab her arm and try to explain. His explanation might be more lies. She didn't know how to wade through to the truth. She didn't know anything right now.

She rushed from her office, down the stairs, and to the daycare hallway, glancing over her shoulder but he didn't follow. Lucky. Or miserably unlucky. She couldn't sort it all out right now, she was too upset and felt too betrayed. Beck marrying her for money was a pain worse than she'd ever known, even with Mark. What she had with Mark had only ever been infatuation. With Beck, she'd fallen so hard she was sure every bone was now broken. She loved him. Desperately. And he'd just shattered her trust and her heart along with it.

She was able to fake it well enough to get Paisley from the kids' club, with only minimal questioning glances from Abbie, and quickly leave through the back entrance of the gym. Paisley kept asking where Beck was but Eve couldn't even answer her.

A few minutes later, she was surprised to find herself in her Cherokee with no sign of Beck chasing her. It just confirmed all of her fears. If he loved her, if he was innocent, he would've chased her down and explained it all.

Tears streaked down her face as she turned on Paisley's favorite kid rock station and handed her daughter her phone to play with. She couldn't go home. Too many memories there of Beck and too much risk of him going there.

She turned east toward Denver on Highway 58. She'd go to Caleb and Emily's. She didn't know if she could tell them the truth either, but maybe she'd stay with them or maybe she'd have her dad send his jet and she'd go to Jackson Hole. The house had just been renovated after the fire last year and her parents had been begging her to come visit.

She should go home and pack a bag but it would be easier to go to a store and buy what they needed than chance Beck coming after her. She'd have her gym manager take over for her. She should put more trust in him anyway. He'd be happy with the opportunity to prove himself.

Eve gripped the steering wheel. The music, the noises from Paisley's game, and Paisley's happy chatter all bounced around and off of her but none of them computed. She couldn't even tell what song was on.

She should be glad that she had a plan: get to Caleb's and then get to Jackson Hole. But nothing felt right. Nothing felt right without Beck. No. She couldn't think like that. He'd lied to her for money just like Mark had. She was running from Beck.

As tears slid down her face, she started wondering if she was insane. She had an incredible man professing his love and because of a misunderstanding, she was running away. It was a pretty huge misunderstanding and with her past marriage, it hit far too close to home. Maybe she just needed some distance from the situation and from Beck, then she could see more clearly. If that logic was sound then heading to Jackson Hole and the safety of her parents was the perfect idea. She'd get away with Paisley on a little vacation. She'd have time to process and know how to proceed with Beck. Yet Beck wouldn't be there. Without him around she felt empty and lethargic.

She pushed it all away and drove. Ten more minutes and she'd be at Caleb's house. He and Emily could help her sort this out. If she got brave enough to even share. She'd always been the quiet one, the one who didn't make a stir, complain, or get too excited about anything. She knew her family would be more than happy to listen to any story she'd share. Then they'd get mad for her, support her, help her talk through this, and figure out what was right for her. Sadly, she hadn't even trusted her own family with Mark's deception as she insisted on doing everything on her own: raising Paisley, putting herself through college, and running her own gym. She always did it herself. Never wanting to burden anyone, even though she knew they didn't look at it like that. They all tried to be around and help her as much as she'd allow.

Since Mark, she'd never fully trusted anyone. Not even her own family... until Beck. She'd given him her trust, her love, and relied on him completely.

At that moment her phone rang. The phone display on her dash said it was Beck. She quickly pushed the end call button on the screen in front of her before Paisley could answer the phone in her hands. Immediately, she regretted pushing it. She wanted to hear his voice. She wanted to hear what he had to say. She really wanted to stop driving and bang her head against the steering wheel. She hated her weakness. If only she could turn the car around and beg Beck to marry her, give her a chance, and learn to love her for her and not for the money. She'd work so hard to make him happy.

Gripping the steering wheel, she focused on getting to Caleb's. She wouldn't be weak for a man. Never again.

Beck waited in Eve's office when she stormed past him and headed down the stairs. She was probably going back to work or maybe to get Paisley early. He needed to shower before they went to lunch, but he'd give her some time to calm down. They'd go get lunch and talk this out.

He walked slowly down the stairs from her office so he wouldn't miss Eve. Wherever she'd stormed off to she'd have to come past the staircase, right? He waited for maybe ten minutes. Then he started to get concerned. He headed back to the daycare center. Abbie confirmed that Eve had picked up Paisley ten minutes ago. Had she slipped by him somehow? He ran through the gym and outside, angling for the parking lot. Her black Cherokee was gone.

He pushed her name on his recent call list. It rang once and hung up. He tried a few more times with the same result. She was hanging up on him? He left a message, asking her to call him back so he could explain. He texted the same thing to her phone and then he drove to her house and banged on the door for a while. Nobody home.

Where could she have gone? Why was she ditching him? He thought he'd let her calm down and then he'd tell her the entire story of Papa's ultimatum, but how could he explain if she wouldn't answer his calls? If she was running from him?

He stood in front of her house and tried her phone one more time. It rang and then hung up. He listened to her sweet voice asking him to leave a message and then he spoke into the phone, "Eve..." He raked a hand through his hair and paced the porch. "I'm sorry I didn't tell you about the money earlier. Please call me back so I can explain. I love you so much. Please give me a chance." He didn't know what else to say without breaking down and telling her how desperately he needed her, how he didn't want to be without her. Did she even care?

CHAPTER FIFTEEN

Three days passed. Beck was at Eve's gym every day, working out and praying she'd appear. He'd called, texted, FaceTimed, stalked her house, begged her employees to tell him where she was, tried to get phone numbers or addresses for her family members, which was proving to be more difficult than he'd foreseen. He'd even debated hiring a private investigator to track Eve down. Nothing. Eve had disappeared from his life and he hurt like he hadn't hurt since his parents had died.

He finished his workout, showered, and was walking through the parking lot and almost to his car when a large man approached from the side. Beck looked over and his jaw dropped. "Caleb?" Was this an answer to his prayers?

Caleb stormed his direction. Beck should've recognized the look of a man who was ready to clean his clock but he was too shocked, and excited, to see Caleb. Eve's brother would have some answers for him.

When Caleb's greeting was a fist to his face, Beck's head snapped back and his eyes widened in surprise.

Beck instinctively shoved Caleb away from him. Caleb knocked into Beck's Bugatti and lifted his eyebrows, giving him a smile that said he wanted to brawl. "You think you're so tough and smooth, famous hockey player with your million-dollar car and all the redheads flocking to you?"

Beck was confused. He'd liked Caleb when he met him. Yeah, the guy had attitude and had given him a hard time about dating Eve but he'd seemed like a good guy and Beck thought Caleb had accepted him. Apparently not.

"What are you talking about? Where is Eve?"

"You think I'd tell you?" Caleb stepped up closer and Beck's muscles tightened, ready for whatever punches the guy decided to lob at him. "What did you do to her?"

"Me?" Beck shook his head. "We had a little misunderstanding and she took off, didn't even give me a chance to explain."

Caleb's eyes narrowed. "You hurt my sister, and now you're going to pay."

Beck thought he was ready, but Caleb plowed into him quick and hard. They knocked to the ground and were trading punches, rolling around, grappling for the upper hand, grunting and tossing out belittling remarks at each other, and in his mind really living. He hadn't had a good fight since last hockey season; pummeling Eve's loser ex didn't count as the man hadn't fought back. This evenly matched slugfest was exactly what Beck needed. All the worry over Eve and the frustration over not being able to find her, talk to her, love her, poured out as he executed hard, vicious hits at her brother's face and upper body, and received his own fair share of future bruises. Caleb was one of the toughest guys he'd ever fought. He loved the battle.

He was breathing heavy and relaxed onto his back for half a second when Caleb grabbed his head and slammed it so hard into the asphalt Beck saw black for a second.

Caleb sat back and scowled at him. "You had enough?"

Beck groaned and rolled up to a seated position. He noticed a small crowd had gathered. He waved and said, "No worries. We're having fun."

"Fun?" Caleb looked like he wanted to brawl all over again. "Messing with my sister is fun for you?"

Beck jumped to his feet and offered Caleb a hand up. Caleb batted it away and stood, glowering at him. Beck wondered if he looked as bad as Caleb—scratched, dirty, and ready to do it all over again.

"No, the fight was fun," Beck said.

Caleb chuckled as he knuckled a cut at the corner of his lip. "I do like some things about you."

Beck lifted his hands. "Hey, I don't mind slugging it out again if you want, but I need Eve. Can you please tell me where she's gone?"

Caleb appraised him. "What happened?"

Beck pushed out a breath, glancing around but luckily the people had dispersed. Where to start? "We fell in love and I thought everything was good, but then her ex showed up."

Caleb straightened so fast his back popped. "Her ex? Did you kill him? Oh, why wasn't I here?" he bemoaned. "I want to thump him so bad."

"She hasn't told you *anything*?"

Caleb shook his head tightly. "That girl is an expert at staying quiet and thinking she can do it all herself. Dang youngest child syndrome, right? Tougher than anyone in the family."

Beck had no clue about that. "Only child."

"Let's walk over to the river," Caleb suggested.

They walked the block and settled onto one of the park benches in the shade, watching Clear Creek dance by.

"Did you at least dismantle the ex for me?" Caleb asked.

"Mark," Beck said. "Yeah, I beat him up pretty good."

"Mark. She never even told us his name," Caleb mused. "Do you have a last name so I can hunt him down and tear him apart?"

"What?" Beck angled toward him. "You really don't know anything?" Now he was in a quandary. Eve had told him things she hadn't even shared with her brother who she was obviously close to. It made him feel good that she had shared with him, trusted him, but now he didn't want to betray her trust. Yet he needed Caleb's help to find her again, gain back the trust he'd lost over the mess with the inheritance.

Caleb shook his head tightly; his scraped knuckles whitening as he clenched his fists. "She was on a senior trip one minute and the next she was apparently in Vegas married. We didn't find out about any of it until months later when she started showing. I think the only reason she ever told any of us she'd even gotten married was because she was pregnant with Paisley." He shrugged helplessly.

"Man, that's messed up."

"You're telling me?" Caleb rolled his eyes. "And don't give me that look or get any ideas. Our family is golden, great people, if I do say so myself." He gave Beck his usual cocky smile. "I know Eve loves and trusts us all and you have no clue how hard we all work to be part of her and Paisley's lives, but she's just so private and that guy wounded her, bad. That's why I came here so fired up. Did you hurt her?" He looked like he'd start brawling again. Beck wouldn't mind, but he needed to find Eve not just enjoy fighting her brother.

"I didn't try to. I love her, man. I was upfront with her, treated her well, loved her, but... I messed up." He hung his head.

Caleb slapped him on the shoulder as if they were friends. At least he hadn't punched him again. "What'd you do?"

"I beat up that Mark guy after he tried to kidnap Paisley."

Caleb's eyes got big and he cursed. "That loser tried to kidnap my niece?" he roared. "Where is he now? It's my turn to use him for a punching bag."

Beck smiled despite the angst. "He's locked up, awaiting trial."

"Oh." Caleb slowly deflated, though his blue eyes were still full of fire. "I guess that's good. We could sneak into the jail, hurt him a little, couldn't we? I've hated that loser for so long. He changed my sister, damaged her bad." He glanced at Beck. "I thought you'd brought her back, but... You should've seen her at my house, mopey, and trying to pretend that everything was happy times."

"Is she still at your house? Aren't you in Denver?" Could Eve truly be that close?

"Just south, Cherry Hills, but no, she's gone. So what happened after you thumped the dirt bag?"

Beck's hope of finding Eve and having her back in his arms wilted again. "Well, it was kind of before all that." Beck walked a fine line between betraying Eve's confidence and giving Caleb the story so her brother would take pity on him and reveal where she was. Beck started by telling him all about his grandpa's crazy demands and then how he'd fallen in love with Eve, trying to take it slow because he knew she needed that. He promised he hadn't asked Eve to marry him so he could get the money, it was more impulsive because of the kidnapping attempt and how desperately he loved her. He told Caleb all he wanted was Eve and Paisley in his life, even if the hyenas ate the billions that should've been his to help children in need.

He finished and stared hopefully at Caleb. "So?"

Caleb regarded him for a second then sprung to his feet and pulled his phone out. He pushed a number and paced as the call connected. "Rach? Eve's man needs help."

"Eve's man?" Beck heard the yell from where he was sitting.

"Yeah, calm down, calm down. I'll give you the story but you need to work your magic." Caleb winked at Beck. "Yep, I'm counting on you, my brilliant sis."

Beck's heart was thudding fast and hard. Caleb was on his side. It wasn't nearly as good as Eve in his arms but it was a start. He at least had hope now. He prayed that Eve being in his arms was the next step, and if his angels in heaven cared at all, could it please be a fast step?

CHAPTER SIXTEEN

Over a week had passed since Eve had seen Beck. She was glad to be with her parents, but she missed Beck with a constant ache and she wanted to go home, back to Beck, to her house, to her gym, to the happy, ordinary life she and Beck had developed.

Her parents had no idea she'd fallen in love with Beck. They'd been focused on Paisley and only tried several dozen times to get the story of why she was there and why she was so morose. Her family was used to her being quiet and Paisley ate up their attention. Paisley said far too much about Beck and asked about him far too often, but Eve was able to play it off with her parents that Beck was just a good friend from the gym and she couldn't count how many times she lied to Paisley and promised her daughter that she'd see him soon. Anyone but a five-year-old would see clean through the lie.

One evening, Eve was on a quiet walk through the woods while her parents played with Paisley on the playset. She stewed about missing Beck, wishing she would stop being such a wimp and answer one of his calls or texts, or at the very least read or listen to one of the many messages he'd left. She'd seen glimpses of his texts when they popped up, always asking for her to give him a chance, or apologizing.

She had no answers, but she thought she was ready to go face him. It wasn't fair to not give him a chance. Though she was terrified that he'd dated her, and asked her to marry him, for all the wrong reasons, she still wanted to talk it out with him. Would she be able to see in his eyes if he was being truthful? If he loved her like she loved him? She prayed hard that she would.

As she walked back to the house she resolved that it was time to go home. Her parents would understand. Maybe she'd even confide in them and get their advice. They were logical, smart, faith-filled people and they'd be thrilled for any chance to help her. They might have insight for her.

She heard voices on the back patio and as she approached she was pleasantly surprised to see Rachel and Abe with her parents and Paisley. There was also some older gentleman that she didn't recognize. Paisley was in Rachel's arms talking away. Rachel looked beautiful with her long, dark hair in curls and her beautiful face beaming at Paisley. Eve thought the scars made Rachel even more beautiful, showed how tough and resilient she was. If only Eve could be as tough as the sister that she idolized. They were different, Eve recognized that. But now that Mark was arrested, Eve didn't need to be so afraid of the media catching a picture of Paisley and maybe she could be brave and be the woman who could stand by Beckett Tanner's side.

They all turned as Eve approached and her dad smiled at her. "Sweetheart. This is Jacob Tanner... Beckett Tanner's grandfather. He'd like to speak with you."

Eve felt the ground shift. She looked into Beck's grandfather's blue eyes and felt a jolt of recognition. He wasn't as tall or broad as Beck but there were some definite similarities, including the dimples in his wrinkled cheeks that grew as he smiled. He walked slowly forward with the aid of a cane, extending his other hand. "Eve Jewel. I've been looking forward to this." He was old, maybe late eighties but he seemed spry and his eyes twinkled at her.

"Thank you, sir." She offered her hand and he held on to it.

"None of this "sir". I think you should call me Papa."

Eve blinked at him. "Um, I'm not sure about that."

"Well, I am." He turned to her family. "Can you give us a few minutes?"

They all nodded except for Paisley who put her little hands on her hips. "If you promise me I see my Beck soon."

Jacob nodded. "I promise, little Princess."

Paisley beamed. "Hey! Beck calls me Princess too."

Jacob grinned. "I raised the boy right."

Rachel looked to Eve. "You're okay?"

Eve nodded. She watched her family walk into the large great room. The windows were two-story and encompassed the entire room to give the view of the forest beyond so they could all watch her and Beck's grandpa if they wanted to.

Eve gestured to the patio chairs. Jacob sank into one and she sat perpendicular to him on a couch.

"You're pretty good at keeping things from your family, aren't you, pretty lady?" he asked.

Eve pursed her lips. "I deal with things on my own and don't burden them."

"That's... dumb. You've got a great family. You should trust them."

He paused as if to let that sink in. Eve knew she had a great family but she was private, what was wrong with that? How much did her family know? She liked her privacy but at the same time, she was sick of never sharing with anyone. She'd been able to share with Beck. What did this mean for her and Beck? His elderly grandfather. Traveling all this way. Had Beck sent him? Could it be possible he loved and ached for her like she loved and ached for him? Yet if that was true why hadn't he come himself?

"You should also trust Beckett," he said.

Eve froze. She should've known he'd get there quick. "I want to," she said softly, "but I'm not sure why he initially started dating me, or why he proposed to me so quickly." She waited with bated breath. Would his grandfather be blunt with her? That was what she wanted.

Jacob sighed heavily. "I demanded Beckett get married by August sixteenth, or all the billions of dollars he should inherit would go to the Save the Hyenas Foundation."

"Save the…" This was a serious subject for her she couldn't help but laugh. "Hyenas?"

He grinned. "I had to think of something really awful to spur him to find the right woman, stop messing around with empty-headed bimbos. I wanted him to find someone like you."

"So he did only date me to save his fortune."

It wasn't a question but Jacob shook his head fiercely anyway. "No. The boy doesn't care about money! He drives a two million dollar car like it's a mini-van. You really think he's caught up on money?"

Eve put a hand to her throat. She'd known his car was nice but… "Two million?" she said faintly.

Jacob chuckled. "That one-of-a-kind car should be in a climate-controlled showroom." He shook his head. "My boy isn't caught up on things or concerned with earthly value. He's one in a million."

Eve gave him a faint smile though she agreed. Beck had put a car seat that probably had Cheerios or fruit snacks stuck on it in a two-million-dollar car, multiple times. He'd handed the keys over to valets who could've taken that car on a joy ride. Obviously money didn't mean much to him.

"He wouldn't listen to me," Papa continued. "I knew, just knew he had to get married and soon. My angels in heaven told me. So I gave him the ultimatum. He didn't care. Said he had to put you first." He raised an eyebrow and Eve's heart thudded quicker and quicker. "I know he only wants my money so he can feed children throughout the world," he rolled his eyes. "Boy's got a bleeding heart like nothing I've ever seen." His smile came again. "I'm proud of him, and I really don't want to give my fortune to those ugly hyenas. But I will, I promise I will. My word is my bond."

Eve's own heart had been racing but now it felt like it slammed to a stop. "He wanted to put me before billions of dollars? He only wants the money to help children?" she repeated.

He nodded. "But he told me to give it to the stupid hyenas because he loves you and he wasn't going to push you into marriage."

Eve felt frozen yet full of more excitement than she'd felt in a while. "He said that?" She searched his blue eyes for any deception but saw only sincerity and a grandfather whose grandson was his entire world.

"Yes, he did. You mean more to him than helping millions of starving orphans."

"That makes me feel awful," she said, but she was laughing. This man didn't beat around the bush, and somehow that reassured her that he was sincere.

"Not trying to guilt you into a quick wedding." He winked.

"I can see that."

They smiled at each other for a few seconds then he asked, "The question is, young lady. Do you love my grandson?"

"Yes." There was no reason to hesitate or lie about it.

Jacob gave her a grin that reminded her of Beck. "Well, all right then. Your sister had some ideas that I think we might all want to talk about."

"Rachel is full of ideas," she said.

He took her hand and squeezed it. "I think Beck and I are going to like being part of your family."

"Now you're being a little presumptuous. I said I loved him, I didn't say I'd marry him."

He arched an eyebrow. "So you'd rather billions of dollars be fed to the hyenas, the disgusting villains in the classic Lion King, than the needy children?"

"Of course not." She eyed him up and down. "You wouldn't really do that." She hoped to call his bluff. She loved Beck but marriage still terrified her and was nothing to rush into, even marriage to a man as appealing and good as Beck.

"Oh, yes I would. It would pain me, but I'm a man of my word, just like Beckett is."

Eve bit at her lip. "So I marry Beck on Saturday or the hyenas get the money?"

"Yep. So what's it going to be, Eve Jewel: are you going to choose love and happiness, rescuing children in the process, or loneliness and making the hyenas howl with happiness instead of you?"

Eve didn't answer right away.

"The clock is ticking," Jacob reminded her.

"Don't rush me."

He smiled. "I think we're going to get along just fine."

Eve liked him but she still didn't want to be forced into marriage. No matter how much she loved Beck or how worthy of a cause it might be. She'd rushed the first time and it hadn't turned out so well. She'd rushed things with Beck after he'd saved Paisley from Mark and everything had exploded shortly after. Her natural cautiousness wasn't a bad thing. She wanted to talk a lot of things through with Beck, kiss him, and know if it was right.

Billions of dollars to the hyenas? Yikes. She needed to pray hard, talk things over with her family, and she needed to see Beck. Hopefully, Jacob's angels who had inspired this crazy idea would give her some inspiration because right now all she had was confusion.

CHAPTER SEVENTEEN

Beck thought he would go crazy with the waiting. Caleb and Rachel claimed they were on his side but they still wouldn't tell him where she was and he hadn't talked to either of them in about thirty-six hours. They both had reassured him the last time they talked that they had a plan and it was going to be brilliant. He didn't care about brilliance. He wanted a plan that had Eve and Paisley back with him.

Friday night his phone rang and he snatched it up.

"My boy!" Papa's booming voice came over the line.

"Hi, Papa." Beck went out back and paced his large patio. It was a beautiful summer's eve but he was missing Eve and Paisley, so much he couldn't appreciate much of anything.

"I've got a great solution to your marriage problem."

Beck groaned but asked, "What's that?"

"I met this gorgeous redhead at the grocery market of all places. She's a couple years younger than you, has half a brain, and a bleeding heart. Said she'd marry you tomorrow to save the children. What do you think?"

Beck sank into a patio chair and leaned his head back, sick to his stomach. "No. I love Eve, Papa. I can't marry anyone else, even if you do follow through with the stupid hyenas."

Grandpa laughed. "Okay, then, meet me at Boulder Country Club about two tomorrow. We'll golf, eat dinner, and try to forget about the misery of all your money going to the hyenas. Stupid lovesick sap that you are."

Beck sighed and agreed. He was a stupid lovesick sap. He agreed to meet Papa at two. He enjoyed golfing and wanted to spend time with his grandpa before the old man passed, even if he was giving his money to the hyenas instead of the children. What a jerk Papa was sometimes.

Beck spent a restless night and worked out hard at Eve's gym the next morning. Instead of practicing at the rink, he went for a long, hot run outside, ate a boring lunch by himself, then showered and headed to the golf course. When he pulled up, the valet predictably goggled over his car and promised him he'd treat it with tender care. Beck wanted to tell him it was just a car and only the woman he loved should be treated with such awe and tender care.

He walked inside and was greeted by a gentleman in a suit. "Beckett Tanner?"

"Yes." He shook the man's hand.

"Come with me, sir. It's a pleasure. Your grandfather wanted to meet you through here." Beck thought the guy was acting a little odd, but he went with him.

They walked into a nice room off the main area, next to the restaurant. His grandfather was waiting there with Rachel and her husband Abe. He recognized them from the online photos. They all stood to greet him, grinning like they'd stolen the Stanley Cup and gotten away with it.

"Hey." He walked over and shook Abe's hand, receiving hugs from Papa and Rachel. "You two joining us for golf?"

"No, sir." Rachel laughed. "I wouldn't want to put you all to shame." She winked. "We're here for your wedding."

Beck's heart thudded faster. Eve? He prayed desperately, *Please say they mean Eve.* "Please say you're not here to try to talk me into marrying some redhead."

"Redhead?" Rachel wrinkled her nose. "We're here to give you away to my sister."

Beck's heart threatened to explode out of his chest. "Eve's here? Where?" His gaze was darting around as if she were hiding behind the furniture.

"Calm down." Papa slapped him on the back. "Desperately lovesick sap. She's waiting outside with the rest of her family and the preacher."

Beck turned and hurried for the door.

"Wait!" Rachel called. "You have to put on your suit."

Beck whirled around. "Eve wants to marry me?"

"Yes."

"Who cares about the suit?" He started toward the door again.

"Get the suit on, son," Papa instructed. "Let her know how special she is to you. Women care about this wedding nonsense even if we don't."

Abe chuckled but Rachel silenced him with a look.

"Okay." Beck conceded. "Where's the suit and where do I change?"

Rachel produced a navy suit and brown leather shoes that looked like Beck's. "It's yours. I broke into your house while you were at the gym."

"Oh? Great." But he couldn't stop smiling. He'd changed into a suit and then he was going to hold and kiss Eve. She'd really agreed to marry him? All he could think was he would see her soon. If she was ready to marry him today he'd happily recite vows, but if she needed more time he'd give it to her. All that mattered was Eve and Paisley in his life, no matter how much time it took to get there, no matter if the hyenas ate the money. Eve. He smiled just thinking about seeing her again. The burden of missing her lifted off his shoulders and he was ready to soar with her by his side.

Eve waited very impatiently in a shady spot by a garden fountain, surrounded by all of her family and the preacher from Caleb and Emily's church. There was a small area set up with chairs and a backdrop for the wedding. She hated that she still felt fear and uncertainty. Would being in Beck's arms settle all her fears or would being in Beck's arms cloud her thinking? The pressure to marry him today so they could donate all that money to the children instead of the hyenas was wearing on her.

Was Beck even coming? What would he think of all of this? What if he didn't want to marry her anymore? She had acted pretty crazy running away from him like she had. Would he understand? Did he really love her and hadn't wanted to rush her as his grandfather had insisted?

Mar let out a low whistle and Eve whipped around. Beck strode confidently out the patio doors of the clubhouse and toward them. His eyes sought her out and he stuttered a step. She bit at her lip as he said, "Ah, Eve," and then he was running her direction.

Eve's heart threatened to burst out of her chest. He was here! She started toward him too, gathering up her lacy wedding dress in her hand.

"My Beck!" Paisley raced in front of Eve and held her arms up to Beck.

Beck swooped her off the ground. "Princess Paisley!" He gave her a tight hug but kept hurrying for Eve.

"I've missed you, my Beck," Paisley said.

"You look so pretty, Princess," he told her, but then he reached Eve. He wrapped his free arm around her, pulled her in tight, and kissed her soundly. It was just as she'd hoped, all the fears settled, everything was right now that she was in Beck's arms. She loved him. She wanted to shout it to anyone who would listen, but most of all say it to him loudly, quietly, before she kissed him, after she kissed him. She pushed all the worries aside and deepened the kiss.

Loud whistles and cheers interrupted them. Beck pulled back and searched her gaze. "Eve."

She smiled up at him, her lower lip trembling. Beck's smile slipped and his lovely dimples disappeared. He turned to Seth who was close by. "Can you please hold the little Princess for a minute?"

"Sure."

Seth took Paisley but she cried out. "I want my Beck."

"Just a minute, pretty girl," Beck said, "I need to talk to your mama." He glanced around at the gathered family. "Thank you all for coming today, making the sacrifice to be here for us." He nodded to Isaac in particular. "But..." Eve's stomach dropped at that but. "There isn't going to be a wedding today. I'm not ready." There were gasps and hushed whispers and Eve wanted to crawl in a hole. Beck wasn't ready. Beck didn't want her.

"Excuse us, please." Beck kept an arm firmly around Eve and escorted her around the fountain and toward some beautiful flower gardens. Her family would keep Paisley entertained but she could only focus on Beck's words. No wedding today.

Eve had felt all lit up being close to him again, but now she was sick with worry. Why had he run to her and kissed her as if she were his world when he wasn't ready? Why didn't he want to marry her anymore? He'd told his grandfather the hyenas could keep the money. She loved that he didn't care about the money but now she was so confused.

He stopped when they were far enough away they wouldn't be overheard and turned to her. "Eve... I'm so sorry I didn't tell you right up front about Papa trying to push me into marriage."

She nodded. So they were starting there? "Thank you. I wish I would've known, but..." He'd said he wasn't ready to get married today but he still seemed to want her. She was going to be truthful and convince him how much she loved him. Maybe there'd be a wedding soon. She could respect his need for more time just like he'd been willing to respect hers. "Maybe knowing about the money would've made me run earlier. I'm so sorry I ran away from you rather than working it out. I won't do that again."

He smiled softly and cupped her chin with his hand. "We'll fight things out good and proper and you won't run away?"

She laughed. "That sounds dreadful, I hate confrontation. But yes, I'm done running." She swallowed and asked bravely, "You aren't ready to be married today but do you still... want me?"

Beck's jaw dropped. He blinked quickly at her and said fiercely, "Eve! Of course, I want you! You're all I want." He pointed back to where their family was waiting. "I said I wasn't ready because I'm not going to pressure you. We can take years if you need, but never doubt that I want to be with you, only you." He smiled softly. "And Paisley too."

Eve was blinking quickly but still, the tears were coming. "I love you so much."

He swept her into his arms and kissed her soundly. "I love you too."

She looked at him, so filled with love for this man. He would've waited years... for her. Apparently Jacob's angels did know a thing or two. "We're getting married today," she said firmly.

"The money doesn't matter," he insisted.

"It's not about the money." She kissed him softly. "It's about you and me. I adore you. I don't want to spend one more second apart from you. I want to marry you, this minute."

He kissed her and kissed her and kissed her. When he finally pulled back her hair was a mess, her lips were swollen, and she wanted to never stop kissing him.

His eyes got serious, so blue, and deep and delectable. She was going to stare into those eyes every day of her life. She'd never thought she could be so happy. "Just to make sure—you want to marry me for me, not to give billions of dollars to famished, hungry, sad children who need it desperately instead of the disgusting hyenas who will just turn the savanna into a frat house?"

Eve smiled. "Since you put it so beautifully." She slid her hands up his chest and around his neck. "I love you, Beck. I want to marry you for you. Keeping your crazy grandfather from gifting his fortune to Save the Hyenas is just a side bonus." She went on tiptoes and kissed him. "But I do have to say that I love you even more for wanting to help so many children."

He ran his hands down her back and pulled her flush against him. "You might say there are a lot of reasons to love me."

"You might, but you might also say you're an overconfident hockey star who needs some humbling." He grinned, making his appealing dimples deepen. She loved that she could turn to teasing with him so quickly. Her confidence was restored and she knew without a doubt she could trust Beck, he would love her completely, and she was right where she should be... in his arms.

"I can see that," he said. "Do you know anyone who could humble me?"

"Paisley. She'll put you right in your place. Or Rachel's pretty good at it too."

He laughed and kissed her. Softly at first but the need she felt for him and how much she'd missed him had her pressing even closer to him and deepening the kiss. Her mouth and head filled up with delicious tingles.

When Beck pulled back, he said, "I want to adopt Paisley. What do you think of that?"

She blinked quickly but again had no way to hide the emotion. Beck wouldn't care. He'd love her weepy and tired or happy and radiant. Right now she was weepy, happy, and so in love. "I think she'll be thrilled, and you'll be the best dad in the world."

"What about the best husband in the world?"

She shrugged. "We'll see about that one."

"Let me see if I can convince you." He dipped her back and kissed her passionately.

"Okay you two, your time's up." Caleb's voice interrupted their kissing. "Are we truly having a wedding today or calling it and getting some food? I missed lunch because Rachel demanded I come hungry and promised me the 'most incredible food ever'. Or are you two just going to make out all afternoon?"

Beck lifted her upright and winked. "I guess if we get married we'll get unlimited make-out time."

"For sure." Caleb agreed. "Em, Krew, and I won the bet and we get to keep Paisley for two weeks while you two go to Luke's exclusive island retreat in the Caribbean."

Eve blew out a breath. "Wow. Unlimited make-out time in the Caribbean. It's a pretty good selling point." She winked at Beck. "I guess I will marry you after all."

Beck chuckled, swept her off her feet, and carried her toward her family and his grandfather. "Did I tell you yet how beautiful you look in this dress?"

"No, sir, you didn't." She clung to his neck, grinning like a fool.

Everyone started clapping, cheering, and whistling as they approached. Especially when Caleb announced with both fists in the air, "They're going to get married!"

Beck set her on her feet in front of the preacher and the beautiful wedding backdrop, keeping one arm around her lower back. He leaned in close. "You look beautiful," he said.

"You already said that," she whispered back.

"I want to kiss you and never stop," he murmured against her ear.

"I don't think you said that," she whispered back.

"Shh, I'm trying to listen to our wedding vows," he said in her ear.

Eve laughed so loud the preacher stopped talking. He smiled at them benevolently and said, "Is this going to be one of those weddings?"

"The one where I keep interrupting the vows to kiss my bride?" Beck asked.

The preacher winked and gestured. "If you must."

"Oh, I must." Then Beck was kissing her and thankfully everyone seemed so thrilled for their happiness that they didn't interrupt that kiss or the half a dozen other kisses that they stopped the vows for. Eve had never been so happy.

Thank you for reading Eve and Beck's story! If you enjoyed this fun romance, please keep reading for excerpts of more Jewel Family Romance.

Hugs,
Cami

Jewel Family Romance

Do Marry Your Billionaire Boss
Do Trust Your Special Ops Bodyguard
Do Date Your Handsome Rival
Do Rely on Your Protector
Do Kiss the Superstar
Do Tease the Charming Billionaire
Do Claim the Tempting Athlete
Do Depend on Your Keeper

DO DEPEND ON YOUR KEEPER

Allison darted a glance away from the ocean waves to the person approaching her. One glance became two and then three, and then she was blatantly staring. Now this was a guy she could gawk at all day. He was nice and fit, jogging in a t-shirt and shorts that couldn't possibly hide the broadness of his chest and shoulders and highlighted the nicely-defined lines of his arms and legs. He had dark skin, eyes, and hair, possibly a mix of Italian and Spanish heritage.

He glanced her way and she gave him a welcoming smile. He smiled back and she stopped walking completely. That smile had been the perfect mix of tough guy with a hint of a smirk. This was a guy who could be there for his lady, making her sigh with longing one minute and laugh the next. This man could sweep Allison off her feet, be her perfect fit.

His smile lingered, but he only gave her a manly tilt of the chin before running on past. What had just happened? Why hadn't he stopped?

She whirled around, planted her hands on her hips, and called out, "It's okay, macho man, keep on running. I didn't want to talk to you anyway."

His head darted back to stare at her and then he gifted her with a deep, throaty chuckle. Turning, he walked back to her, stopping a couple of feet away. "Were you speaking to me?"

"No." She gestured around at the couple making out up by the parking lot. "I was yelling at them."

He chuckled again and eased in closer. His dark eyes sparkled mischievously at her. "Apologies, I never would've guessed a woman of your beauty and class would be yelling at random men on the beach."

She hid a smile. "I think you're a few steps above 'random'."

"You don't even know me."

"Whose fault is that?" She tossed her long, dark hair and gave him an inviting smile. She wasn't much good at maintaining relationships, but she was pretty good at flirting with appealing men.

He laughed, loud. She liked that she could make him laugh like that. "I guess it's mine, if I don't do something about it."

"What are you going to do about it?" she challenged. She wouldn't usually be this forward with a man she didn't now, but there was something about him that told her she could trust him. He had that innate protection built into his strong muscles and the handsome lines of his face.

He looked her over slowly. "Get your phone number and ask you on a date?"

She shook her head. "Nope. I don't give my number to strange men and I don't go on dates with someone I just met on the beach."

He shook his head. "I guess it'll be your fault you don't get to know me then."

She debated. She could hear Abe's voice warning her to be smart and careful, but there was something about this guy. She wanted to see him again. "I'll be walking this stretch of beach about the same time tomorrow evening."

"I'll be seeing you then." He gave her a slow grin she felt clear through. This guy could be a lot of fun to flirt with.

Allison gave him one more inviting smile then turned and walked away. She put a little extra sway in her hips, just in case he decided to use that brain of his and watch her go. Glancing over her shoulder she was rewarded to find him not just watching, but soaking her in. His dark eyes seemed to call to her. She forced herself to face north and walk away. It was one thing to flirt with a handsome man on a public beach. It was quite another to invite him into her life too quickly. She'd stay smart and safe, but she'd definitely be walking this stretch of beach tomorrow night, ready to flirt with him some more.

———

Find *Do Depend on Your Keeper* here.

DO TEASE THE CHARMING BILLIONAIRE

Turning, he saw a vision in red and swayed on his feet.

Rachel stood right behind him wearing a long formal dress. Her dark eyes were outlined with smoky makeup and her lips were a deep red that matched the dress. She gave him a welcoming smile and he let himself appreciate the entire exotic effect of her appearance for a minute. The dress was floor length but had a slit on one leg that came well above her knee and showed off enough beautiful tanned leg to make his mouth go dry. Her right shoulder was bare and the dress tucked around her chest on that side. On the left side it covered her shoulder with a capped sleeve but most of the left side of the silky red bodice was covered with her long, dark hair that swooped from her forehead across her cheek and then was pulled forward to cover her neck and chin on the left side. He wished he could help her know she didn't need to cover up, but he could at least tell her how beautiful she was.

"Rachel," he breathed out, automatically extending his hand. "You are exquisite."

She put her hand in his, and just like this afternoon, he was struck by the power that seemed to surge through him at her very feminine touch. He could be her Tarzan or Superman or whoever she wanted him to be when she had her hand in his. He wanted to be more for her. A billionaire from upstate New York who had scrapped his future out of nothing but sheer will and his own two hands wasn't nearly good enough for a woman with such light, intelligence, and grit.

Acting like a sappy charmer, well, like Preston really, he bent low and brought her hand up to his lips. "Beautiful," he said, then remembered that he'd already said she was exquisite. What was he doing? He wasn't here to fall for a woman. In fact, falling for a woman hadn't been on his radar since Angel backstabbed and betrayed him almost ten years ago.

"Thank you." Rachel gifted him with a smile that made her even more appealing. "I didn't figure you for a 'compliments flowing like honey from his tongue' kind of guy."

He laughed and tilted closer to her. "Would you believe me if I told you that I'm usually not?"

"No."

Oh, he liked her sass. Most women were enamored with his success and his looks and either flirted brazenly with him or acted like he was Zeus. Rachel did neither, but at least she did seem interested in him. He caught a glimpse of Preston coming their way and remembered Rachel was supposed to dine with his lifelong friend. He cursed and she lifted an eyebrow.

"Sorry," he muttered. He'd picked up some habits in prison his mom didn't like and swearing was one of them. He lowered his voice as Preston came closer. "Meet me on the beach after dinner?"

Rachel scrunched her nose and tilted her head to the left, her long hair trailing almost to the curve of her waist. "We'll see."

Keep reading here.

ABOUT THE AUTHOR

Cami is a part-time author, part-time exercise consultant, part-time housekeeper, full-time wife, and overtime mother of four adorable boys. Sleep and relaxation are fond memories. She's never been happier.

Join Cami's VIP list to find out about special deals, giveaways and new releases and receive a free copy of *Rescued by Love: Park City Firefighter Romance* by clicking here.

cami@camichecketts.com
www.camichecketts.com

ALSO BY CAMI CHECKETTS

Jewel Family Romance

Do Marry Your Billionaire Boss

Do Trust Your Special Ops Bodyguard

Do Date Your Handsome Rival

Do Rely on Your Protector

Do Kiss the Superstar

Do Tease the Charming Billionaire

Do Claim the Tempting Athlete

Do Depend on Your Keeper

Strong Family Romance

Don't Date Your Brother's Best Friend

Her Loyal Protector

Don't Fall for a Fugitive

Her Hockey Superstar Fake Fiance

Don't Ditch a Detective

Don't Miss the Moment

Don't Love an Army Ranger

Don't Chase a Player

Don't Abandon the Superstar

Steele Family Romance

Her Dream Date Boss

The Stranded Patriot

The Committed Warrior

Extreme Devotion

Quinn Family Romance

The Devoted Groom

The Conflicted Warrior

The Gentle Patriot

The Tough Warrior

Her Too-Perfect Boss

Her Forbidden Bodyguard

Cami's Collections

Strong Family Romance Collection

Steele Family Collection

Hawk Brothers Collection

Quinn Family Collection

Cami's Georgia Patriots Collection

Cami's Military Collection

Billionaire Beach Romance Collection

Billionaire Bride Pact Collection

Billionaire Romance Sampler

Echo Ridge Romance Collection

Texas Titans Romance Collection

Snow Valley Collection

Christmas Romance Collection

Holiday Romance Collection

Extreme Sports Romance Collection

Georgia Patriots Romance

The Loyal Patriot

The Gentle Patriot

The Stranded Patriot

The Pursued Patriot

Jepson Brothers Romance

How to Design Love

How to Switch a Groom

How to Lose a Fiance

Billionaire Boss Romance

Her Dream Date Boss

Her Prince Charming Boss

Hawk Brothers Romance

The Determined Groom

The Stealth Warrior

Her Billionaire Boss Fake Fiance

Risking it All

Navy Seal Romance

The Protective Warrior

The Captivating Warrior

The Stealth Warrior

The Tough Warrior

Texas Titan Romance

The Fearless Groom

The Trustworthy Groom

The Beastly Groom

The Irresistible Groom

The Determined Groom

The Devoted Groom

Billionaire Beach Romance

Caribbean Rescue

Cozumel Escape

Cancun Getaway

Trusting the Billionaire

How to Kiss a Billionaire

Onboard for Love

Shadows in the Curtain

Billionaire Bride Pact Romance

The Resilient One

The Feisty One

The Independent One

The Protective One

The Faithful One

The Daring One

Park City Firefighter Romance

Rescued by Love

Reluctant Rescue

Stone Cold Sparks

Snowed-In for Christmas

Echo Ridge Romance

Christmas Makeover

Last of the Gentlemen

My Best Man's Wedding

Change of Plans

Counterfeit Date

Snow Valley

Full Court Devotion: Christmas in Snow Valley

A Touch of Love: Summer in Snow Valley

Running from the Cowboy: Spring in Snow Valley

Light in Your Eyes: Winter in Snow Valley

Romancing the Singer: Return to Snow Valley

Fighting for Love: Return to Snow Valley

Other Books by Cami

Seeking Mr. Debonair: Jane Austen Pact

Seeking Mr. Dependable: Jane Austen Pact

Saving Sycamore Bay

Oh, Come On, Be Faithful

Protect This

Blog This

Redeem This

The Broken Path

Dead Running

Dying to Run

Fourth of July

Love & Loss

Love & Lies

Made in United States
Cleveland, OH
15 February 2026

33433190R00085